THUNDER IN EUROPE

THE DEPARTMENT Z SERIES

THUNDER IN EUROPE

DEPARTMENT Z

JOHN CREASEY

OPEN ROAD
INTEGRATED MEDIA
NEW YORK

Copyright © 1936 by John Creasey

ISBN: 978-1-5040-9198-5

This edition published in 2024 by Open Road Integrated Media, Inc.
180 Maiden Lane
New York, NY 10038
www.openroadmedia.com

This book is dedicated to
THE GENTLEMEN AT GENEVA
and with it thanks for their past labours, hopes* for their future
unceasing efforts, and faith in their eventual achievement.

JOHN CREASEY, *1935*

* In vain, as it turned out.
J.C.—1968

THUNDER IN EUROPE

1

THE MAN WHO CAME BACK

Very few people who passed the office in Whitehall known cryptically as Z knew Gordon Craigie, that great gentleman whose duty it was, time after time, to send men to die.

It has been said, with truth, that those men had died with a smile on their lips, the thought of Craigie's steadfast eyes giving them courage. It is as true that no man stepped across the threshold of Department Z who was not prepared to go to the ends of the earth for Craigie. There was something in his lean face that filled men with a tremendous zest for England, and the peace and goodwill that England stood for. Day in, day out, Craigie was at Whitehall, reading reports from agents throughout the world, carefully and laboriously fitting together pieces of the puzzles that perpetually threatened the safety of his country and world peace. Messages reached him in diverse ways and in various disguises, telling of things that no other man in England would have believed. He sifted them, until he found what was true, and what false.

If he had ever spoken one tenth of what he knew, the

countries of the world would have been at each other's throats, and the God of War would have laughed again. But Craigie did not talk. Even those for whom he worked learned only as much as he thought wise to tell; and the things he kept secret made his hair a little greyer, and the lines at his eyes more pronounced.

One bleak morning in March, Craigie left his Brook Street flat, which for once he had visited overnight, and walked briskly towards Whitehall. It was eight o'clock, and the first shivering workers were sprinkling the bare spaces of the West End with watery eyes and cold, blue skin. Craigie, dressed in a trilby and a long mackintosh, went easily onwards, feeling refreshed by the cold air.

He divided his year into two seasons, winter and summer. It was time, now, to take stock of the winter, to see what had happened, to find which men had gone from England on strange missions, and who had failed to return. And bleaker by far to Gordon Craigie than the wind was the prospect he saw. Many men had gone, as many in that half year as would normally disappear in twelve full months. He knew that, even before he reached the office and checked this man's departure and that man's return.

He viewed the prospect logically. If his heart bled for those who disappeared, the bleeding must not reach his mind.

There were rumours of war in the East and West. There were trade pacts and armament pacts, secret, vicious things, and if an agent of Department Z had scented one and followed its trail and had been caught, it was no use debating what had happened to him. It was a time, Craigie knew, when Intelligence casualties were growing, for each Power was suspicious of its friendliest neighbour.

Hence the long list of men who had left Whitehall but had not returned.

Craigie reached his office at half past eight. A little curl of smoke came from the embers of yesterday's fire, in the grate, for Craigie had been in the office until the early hours. He rekindled the fire, left the office again to collect the basket of post that would be waiting for him in the room of a Very High Official. At Whitehall, no one ever lent a hand in the running of Department Z. Craigie was its sole representative there, from office boy to director.

The post was small. Less than a dozen letters waited for him. He took them back, smiled with satisfaction when he saw the fire was burning merrily, and opened the envelopes.

His eyes hardened as he read.

He knew the prevailing code so well that he could decode his letters on sight. It was strange that four letters from mid-European states held a similar message. Craigie assembled them in chronological order. In his precise handwriting he made entries in a book that at times held the secrets of the world between its covers. The entries, extracts from the four letters, read thus:

'Vienna contact reports Carris here in November. No further trace.'

'Moscow contact reports Carris called in January. Movements since not known.'

'Leningrad contact reports Carris here January.'

'Riga contact states Carris left here February after seven days' stop.'

Craigie finished other entries, until the whole of his post was summarised in the book. Then he burned the letters, closed the book and left it on the large, bare desk at one end of the office. Slowly he walked to the fire and sat in a large, comfortable but worn leather armchair. Automatically he took a deep-bowled meerschaum from its rack fixed in the wall, stuffed it with thick twist, and started to smoke. Every movement was slow and deliberate. He acted like a man in a trance, although he was actually concentrating every thought on the problem in hand—the question of Nick Carris.

Carris was one of the few agents who had been with Department Z for over ten years. Most agents retired from the service before that period had elapsed, or had died in it. But Carris had borne a charmed life.

What was more remarkable was that Carris had left the office over a year before, had made two reports, and then stopped communicating. Craigie had long since given him up for lost. Now, unexpectedly, he was on the trail again; but he had not contacted Craigie.

Why?

Carris was more than reliable—he was a brilliant agent. There was some good reason for his failure to get in touch, and an equally good one for his contact with the four cities without leaving a message to be passed on. There was one possible explanation—Carris had cause to believe that a message left in the hands of his European contacts would not be safe; he had, therefore, signalled his activity without giving anything away.

Craigie went over the agent's movements again and again. Vienna, Moscow, Leningrad and Riga were all dangerous places for a Department Z agent. Probably more men had disappeared from Russia than any other country, and Carris was apparently working the Soviet. He had left on a roving commission, bound to no district and no instructions. And as his last contact had been at the Latvian capital it was possible that he was making for England now, by way of the Baltic.

The one thing certain, Craigie told himself, was that Carris had found something which he would describe as hot. Things were always cold, cool or hot to Nick Carris, and he would not have covered himself so carefully for a cool breeze. Something hot, something big.

Craigie ran his mind over the possibilities as he began to refill his pipe. There was little use in guessing, but . . .

As he put a light to his pipe, something flickered in front of him, a faint green light in the middle of the mantelpiece. He shook the match out and went to the side of the room. With a slight pressure of his thumb on a spot in the light oak panelling, he set the sliding panel into motion. The panel revealed a solid oak door, which he opened. In the semi-darkness of the passage beyond there was nothing to be seen. Craigie went along the passage until he reached the top of a flight of stone steps that led into the roomier quarters of the Government building.

Halfway up the steps a man was standing.

Craigie had expected him; his surprise was that the caller had reached the stairs without coming farther. No man could have operated the lever that had shown the green light without possessing the full qualifications of a Department Z agent, and few agents hesitated to come as far as they could.

Then Craigie's face hardened as he hurried towards the man on the steps, reaching him and putting a supporting arm about his shoulders.

'Take it easy,' he said. 'There's no hurry.'

The man said nothing. Craigie felt his weight, very heavy against his arm. The man was almost lifeless; how he had made that journey through the stone passages of the building without attracting attention, and therefore help, was beyond the Chief of Department Z. He heard the other's breath, short, panting gasps; what was worse, he saw the other's face.

He knew the man for an agent of Z. No other could have pressed that control. But Craigie knew every one of his agents by sight, yet did not recognise this one. The man's face was one great scar, red, ugly, as if he had been plunged head first into a blazing fire. There were no lashes to his eyes, no brows, no hair. His lips were shapeless and his nose crushed.

'Steady,' murmured Craigie. 'We're nearly there. Another couple of yards.'

They stepped into the office. Craigie slid the moving panel into position while his caller slumped back against the wall, breathing between lips that made just a gash across his fire-red face.

'Over here,' said Craigie.

He half carried his man to the armchair, settled him in it, turned to a cupboard near the fireplace and took out a brandy flask. He set it to the other's lips. The man swallowed, gasped and shuddered. For the first time his eyes opened, those eyes with the lashes burned off and the lids a mass of scars.

Then Craigie saw and recognised him. No two men could have those piercing blue eyes.

'I'm glad you're back, Nick,' he said, and his voice was steady enough to surprise himself.

For the first time in his life Craigie was welcoming back an agent he had given up for lost—and who he was wishing had never returned. Nick Carris, like this. Carris, tall, lithe, handsome, with his fine flashing eyes and his quick smile, looks that could have turned the heads of a hundred women, if Carris had wanted it. Nick Carris, scarred, unrecognisable, a travesty of a man.

It turned Craigie sick.

It was horrible, looking in the living blue eyes of a face that was otherwise dead and motionless. If there was an expression in those eyes, Craigie thought, it was a grim, bitter humour. Carris knew what his chief was thinking.

'I'm glad you're back,' Craigie said again.

Carris swallowed hard and opened his lips. He could hardly move them apart, for the muscles of his face were stiff and set. But it was Carris's voice.

'I'm not,' he said.

'Idiot,' said Craigie, with a ghost of a smile. It wouldn't do to talk differently from the way he had talked to Carris a hundred times before.

'Idiot,' said Carris. His whole face moved as he spoke. It was like looking at a swollen, shiny mask, with lips opening and shutting as if they were jerked by a string. 'Maybe. I haven't got long, thank God. Didn't think I'd get here.'

'Hmm,' said Craigie.

'Hell of a job,' said Carris. He fumbled in his pockets and drew out a crumpled packet of cigarettes. 'Everyone who saw me shied off. Poor devils. Don't blame 'em.'

Craigie lit the cigarette for him.

'Got a bit of lead,' Carris said, as he let the smoke curl out of his mouth. 'Lodging in the lung, I think. Damned near impossible to breathe. That side.'

'Hmm,' said Craigie. Not by word nor deed did he reveal his thoughts, his pity for Nick Carris. 'Carry on while I telephone. I can hear you.'

'You always could do two things at once.' Carris essayed a mockery of a grin. 'Not much to tell. Only this, Craigie. Watch that swine, Krotz. I swore I'd tear him to pieces after he'd done this.'

Carris lifted his hand to his face. Only his blue eyes stared straight ahead of him, burning bright as ever.

'I'll watch him,' promised Craigie, as he reached his desk

and lifted up the telephone. 'So it's a Lathian job?'

'Don't know,' said Carris. 'Krotz is such a double-crossing swine, he'd sell his country, president or not. He's doing something. Big. I don't know what. I've followed him all over Europe.'

'Send a doctor up to me, please,' said Craigie into the telephone. As he replaced it: 'So that's why you left contact, but not a message?'

'Yes. Daren't say anything. Krotz was having me watched. He knew I was on his tail. Tried to scare me off twice. Then . . .' Again the sick man's hand went towards his face. 'Vitriol. God knows how it didn't blind me. Krotz did it.'

'I'll fix him,' murmured Craigie, back at his seat opposite the other. 'Don't talk too much. You want to save your strength.'

'Why? I'm finished. Iron constitution only—all that tripe— kept me going. Doctor's no good. Think I want to live looking like this?'

'Steady,' said Craigie.

'Might as well enjoy my last minutes.' Carris coughed, suddenly, and then Craigie saw blood on his lips. It was impossible to judge how bad Carris was from that death-mask of a face. 'Can't ask anything more. Lived for Z as long as I can remember. Dying in the office. Record, eh?' He leaned forward suddenly, and his hand shot out, a lean, strong hand with a vice-like grip that lasted only for a fraction of a second on Craigie's forearm. 'Gordon—whoever takes on my job—tell 'em not to let Krotz breathe a second more than they must. He's done worse to others than he has to me. *Worse!*'

The grip relaxed, and Carris dropped back in his chair with his eyes closed. Craigie reached towards him and stripped off his coat, carefully, gently. The vest followed it. The shirt was covered with brown-drying blood on the left side. Craigie took out a knife and began to cut the fabric away from the wound.

Carris sat there like a dead man, while Craigie bathed the ugly, congealing hole with tepid water, cleansing it as best he could. The wound was at least twelve hours old. If it had been attended to before it might have healed, but now . . .

'Got it in Paris,' the agent said, unexpectedly. His eyes opened again and that bitter humour was in them. 'One of Krotz's men. Read about him tomorrow. I shot him and he dropped into the Seine. Came over by air. Knew I could just manage to make it. Message might have—gone astray.'

'You didn't,' said Craigie gently.

'Not likely.' Carris twisted his lips into that ghastly smile again. 'Last trip, old boy. By the way, nine months in Siberia. Krotz trumped up a charge. Krotz . . .'

Carris stopped for a moment and Craigie, looking down at him, saw his eyes blazing with a fierce light. Eyes that had laughed, mocked and challenged their way across the world were like blue fire, with hate.

'Get him,' muttered Nick Carris. 'Get him, Gordon. Make him die slowly. Make him suffer. Imagine it. Vitriol. Burning, burning, and nothing to help, just him laughing. Get him, Craigie—Krotz!'

Craigie's hands rested on his shoulders. Carris's body was writhing—until, suddenly, all movement stopped.

Craigie looked down in infinite sadness at the face which was scarred out of recognition. Then his lips tightened.

'I'm afraid,' he said, five minutes later, 'you're too late, Doctor. Sorry. Will you take a look at him?'

But Craigie knew that Nick Carris had died for the thing that had been life to him, and he had died voicing hatred of the man who had made him suffer such agonies.

Krotz.

2

THE MAN WHO WAS CURIOUS

J ust after two o'clock that March day, the reading-room of
the Carilon Club, last stronghold of Man in London, was
comparatively deserted. As some indication of the
manner of the three men who graced it, the three large
windows were wide open and the men sat or lounged near
them. The room was cold. In an hour's time the old brigade
would storm in, with newspapers, cigars, anecdotes, and eventually, in the stertorous somnolence of mid-afternoon, the
windows jammed tight, in the atmosphere would be what Jim
Burke would call a fug. But until that invasion came, the air
was icy and the three occupants enjoyed it.

To the right and left of Burke, who was deep down in an
armchair large enough to engulf even his vast form, were
Timothy and Toby Arran. Timothy, exquisite of dress and
feature, was lounging against the open window, and at that
moment was placing a screwed ball of paper on his left thumb.
As it balanced he flicked it skilfully towards Burke. It flashed
past that worthy's eyes, but for all the effect it made it might
have flashed past stone.

Toby Arran, reputed the ugliest man in London, stooped, picked the ball from the carpet, placed it in turn on his thumb and flicked. It struck plumb on the side of a substantial nose.

'What the . . .' began Burke, and then he saw Toby's grinning face. He dropped the book in which he had been immersed to his knees and regarded Toby sorrowfully.

'Parasites,' he said. 'Both of you. Get to blazes out of here and let me finish this book, or . . .'

'Little man, don't swear,' chided Timothy.

'It must be that he's reading all about love.'

'Useless wastrels,' said Burke.

'It's the beautiful originality of the man that makes me fond of him,' murmured Timothy. 'The lovely selection of words and phrases, too.'

'Delightful to hear,' agreed Toby, solemnly.

Burke regarded them in turn and grinned. His tanned face was illuminated by a flash of white teeth, and his grey eyes took on a thousand wrinkles.

'What a pity it is,' he murmured, 'that you can't play billiards. Funny, some people handle a cue like a pick-axe.'

'Who can't handle a cue?' demanded Toby, who was proud of his prowess.

'You can't,' said Burke rudely, 'and Tim's worse.'

'I'll give you fifty in a hundred,' said the twins—for they were the Arran twins, sometimes called the Unholy—as in one breath.

'I'll play the both of you,' scoffed Burke, closing his book and resting it on the side of his chair. 'We'll have a poke a piece, and my total at the end of half an hour will be bigger than yours together. Much bigger.'

He eased himself out of his chair and stalked towards the door of the billiard room, leading from the reading-room. They reached the door of the billiard room together, and

Burke, with exaggerated courtesy, bowed for them to pass him. They passed, still breathing vengeance. And as Timothy disappeared, Burke helped him with a shove, pulled the door with a bang, and turned the key in the lock. There was a moment of stupefied silence on the far side of the door, and then:

'You pesty swindler!' bellowed Toby.

'Of all the . . .' began Timothy.

'What you have received,' said Burke, as he walked back to his chair and his book, 'you have surely asked for. Have a nice little game. I'll let you out in half an hour.'

These things tend to show something of the nature of the Arrans, and a great deal of the nature of James William Burke.

There were people who guessed Burke's age to be twenty-five, and others who hazarded thirty-five; both estimates were wrong, for he was thirty. In those thirty years he had crammed a great deal of experience. He had lived, loved, barged his way through a hundred tight corners, and had emerged from all his encounters with his grin as wide and spontaneous as ever, his temper—like that of many big men—very even, his muscles trim, his constitution genuinely like that of an ox, and an appetite for many more experiences in the line of violence, but none in the ways of love. He had been bitten twice. No one could have called him handsome, but the sweeping lines of his chin bespoke strength. His nose was larger than it should have been, but was straight and shapely. His lips were wide, curving and easy in laughter, as were his grey, lazy eyes. His hair was fittingly dark and crisp. He had a pair of immense shoulders, proportionately slim hips, arms and legs worthy of his deep chest and a heart that erred on the side of being generous.

He had a working knowledge of most countries in the world, languages enough to get him through any emergency, and a curious lack of the stiffness that characterises Englishmen abroad. On that March day he was spending his first full day in England for three months, and he was finishing a book he had started on the plane from Paris. He didn't know it, but he had preceded Nick Carris by some eight hours.

He turned the last pages, lit a cigarette, and listened to hear the click of balls in the billiard room. He was contemplating whether to let the Arrans have another ten minutes in captivity when the door opened from the main hall and an attendant looked in.

He looked surprised.

'Looking for?' asked Burke.

'Mr. Timothy Arran, sir. They must have slipped out.'

'They're in the billiard room,' said the big man. 'I'll take that in to 'em.'

The note, which Burke saw in the man's hand, was passed over. Burke joined the twins as Timothy was making a *massé* shot; he brought it off, with a grunt.

'Good one,' said Burke.

'Like to try and play me?' demanded Timothy.

'I play,' said Burke, grinning, 'by design.'

The subtlety of this, however, was lost, as Timothy played a red loser too thinly, and Toby applauded. Burke handed the note over.

'I'll take your cue,' he offered.

Timothy relinquished it without a word. Burke watched Toby shape for his shot and caught the expression in Tim's eye. What he saw surprised him. In that moment Timothy looked excited, a tense inward excitement that Burke would not have credited him with.

'Missed it,' grunted Toby.

Burke forgot Timothy's expression and finding the balls

15

running well for him, made a break of twenty-seven, to the accompaniment of remarks from Toby that were not all congratulatory.

'Now *I'll* show you how to play billiards,' promised the ugly twin. But he was doomed to disappointment, for Timothy said:

'Have a look at this, Toby.'

Burke looked at him sharply. The big man was not curious by nature, but Tim's earlier excitement had intrigued him. Now he saw the other's face drawn, with a hardness in his eyes that he had never seen before.

Toby took the letter and read it quickly.

The expression on his face changed from one of faint amusement to a drawn, tense look that matched his brother's. Whatever the letter brought, it was certainly bad news.

'Hmm,' said Toby, after a long pause. 'Well, I suppose we should have expected it.'

'It's been coming for a long time. But it's a devil for Pat.'

They remembered, suddenly, that Burke was there. It was Timothy who looked at the big man, with a faint grin, and spoke in a curiously hard voice.

'Sorry, Jim, but we'll have to leave you.'

'Nothing too bad, I hope,' said Burke.

'Vile,' Timothy said. 'You knew Nick Carris, didn't you?'

'A nodding acquaintance, yes.'

'He's dead,' said Timothy. 'We'll have to tell his sister, and it's not a job we like.'

The change from the idle pleasantries of a few minutes before to the grimness of death was disconcerting. Burke put his cue up slowly.

'Don't see how I can help,' he said.

The twins shook their heads, and turned towards the door. Timothy was folding the letter up as he turned, and he jarred against his brother's arm. The letter fluttered to the floor, opening as it went, and for a moment Burke saw it.

A peculiar sensation assailed him as he glanced down.

The letter was from friends of the man Carris, telling the Arrans of his death. So much they had told him. But the letter was from a well-known firm of food exporters in London; so much the letter-heading told him.

So it looked very much as if they had lied.

Yet there was no reason why they should have done. Nor was there any possibility of mistaking the expression on their faces. But why, in Heaven's name, should news of a man's death be sent on business letter-heading? Burke noticed something else, too. Timothy dived for that letter quickly, as if he was afraid the big man had seen it, and tucked it safely into his pocket.

'No,' he admitted, 'I don't see there's anything you can do. But thanks.'

He waved his hand, and Burke responded. The door closed behind the twins, while Burke leaned against the billiard table very thoughtfully.

He had heard rumours that the Arran twins were not always what they appeared to be. They seemed very much what he had called them—useless wastrels. Apparently they did nothing but lounge or play, they had no direct interest in life, and they had even kept free from marriage. But there was a rumour that Toby Arran had fallen in love with a Parisian dancer while in Paris on 'holiday'. The dancer had been murdered, and for a while nothing had been seen of the Arran twins, but later there had been some talk of a fight near Godalming. Burke knew little of the story, but it was enough to make him wonder how Toby had met his dancer, and whether the rumour of the Godalming fracas had its roots in plain fact.

It was the kind of rumour that intrigued Burke. He rubbed his chin very thoughtfully as he moved towards the door, hurried through the stately passages of the Carilon Club and reached the courtyard. The Arrans' Frazer Nash was disappearing into the Mall, and a taxi was coasting behind it.

Burke whistled the cabby and hurried towards it. He reached it, wrenching the door open before the driver had brought the car to a halt.

'The Frazer Nash in front,' he said tersely.

Automatically the cabby speeded up; he scented money if he caught up with the Frazer Nash. He contrived it, across Trafalgar Square, up Haymarket, along Regent Street, towards Edgware Road and Marylebone. In one of the turnings off the Marylebone Road the Frazer Nash disappeared, and as the taxi passed the turning, Burke saw the Arrans climbing out of their stationary car. The house where they were calling was less than twenty yards down the street, Lord's Avenue.

The cabby pulled up on the far side of the avenue.

' 'Ere you are, sir.'

'Five times one,' said Burke with a very straight face, 'is five. Here's one pound. Hang on here indefinitely and the chance of making it five might come.'

'Oke,' said the cabby, fingering the note. 'I'll be 'ere all day, sir, if yer wants me.'

'Turn into the avenue, will you, and keep your eye on that car? Two men came out of it. See how many come back from the house to the car.'

'Oke,' repeated the cabby, economically.

Burke slipped away.

He had no desire to be seen by the Arrans, certainly not until he had discovered a great deal more than he had. He could rely on the cabby, and that it did not matter if he did miss anything in Lord's Avenue—nothing was likely to happen in the street.

He explored the Marylebone Road where it faced the avenue and was disappointed by the absence of any café or shop where he might reasonably linger while keeping the Frazer Nash under survey. A draper's establishment seemed unsuitable. A hairdresser's was ruled out because he would probably be shoved into a cubbyhole, and for half an hour lost to the world. A coal-order office had possibilities, but would not guarantee shelter for more than five minutes. The safest bet, for the first few minutes, was a tobacconist's directly opposite the turning.

He was turning over in his mind a selection of names of cigarettes that the tobacconist would certainly not stock, when he saw the dark-skinned man slouch into Lord's Avenue and walk towards the Frazer Nash. In Burke's makeup there was no prejudice against men with dark skins, but there was a big question mark against any man who stopped by a stationary car.

The man leaned over the side of the Frazer Nash. From where he stood, Burke saw the other pull papers from the dashboard recess, stuff them in his pocket and move off quickly. It was all over in a flash.

'And yet,' murmured Burke, 'the Swarthy One has now what he didn't have a minute ago, and shouldn't have at all.'

Burke thought quickly. Should he wait for the Arrans to come out of the house, or follow the dark-skinned man?

The latter was slouching back towards the Marylebone Road. Burke ran his eyes over him. Sharp features, eyes too close together and downcast, very thin body and flashy clothes completed the picture.

'I'll know him again,' muttered Burke to himself. 'Better stick to the Arrans.'

A solution to his problem flashed, literally, in front of his eyes. A policeman passed him.

'Officer,' called Burke pleasantly. 'A job for you. I saw that man, turning out of Lord's Avenue, take something from a car.'

'Did you, then?' said the policeman.

Secretly, Burke applauded the man, who looked behind him, saw a second constable within twenty yards, motioned towards the swarthy-faced man, and then walked quickly away from Burke.

Smiling grimly, the latter waited and watched.

The policeman he had addressed passed his quarry while on the opposite side of the road. The second man passed Burke. Together they walked quickly across the thoroughfare, and before Swarthy Face had realised what was happening, he was hemmed in.

Burke couldn't hear what passed. He could imagine the thief's sullen protest, and he was waiting for the man to be brought across to him. They actually started, the thief gripped firmly by each arm . . .

Then the Daimler saloon crossed Burke's vision.

He saw that its curtains were drawn, but it did not occur to him there was any motive behind that. The first intimation he had of tragedy was a high-pitched scream from the other side of the road! Then the Daimler flashed by.

The prisoner was falling, an ugly splotch of red across his forehead. A policeman's helmet was whirling to the pavement, one constable was leaning back against the window of a shop, the other staring in stupefaction at the vanishing Daimler. In that fraction of a second this thing had happened—machine-gun fire in the Marylebone Road!

Then came uproar.

A woman screamed and a man shouted. A policeman some distance away blew blast after blast on his whistle, people scurried to and fro frantically, a boy was standing pop-eyed on the kerb, a motorist jammed on his brakes as half a dozen men raced towards the two policemen and their captive.

Burke didn't see how he could help. There were a dozen others nearer the wounded man than he. And if he had been curious about the Arrans before, he was burning with it now. The thief had acted under orders by robbing the Arrans' car. He had been watched, his arrest had been seen, and to make sure that he didn't talk to the police, he had been shot. It was cold-blooded; but it was logical.

A dozen questions hammered against his mind as he slipped into the hairdresser's. It was wiser to lose himself completely, and that was the surest means of doing it.

'A trim,' he said to the white-smocked man who came from the rear of the shop.

'This way, sir.'

Burke followed his guide and suffered the preparations for a haircut. The man was not talkative, and Burke was able to think.

It might be possible that the thief had chosen the Arrans' car by chance, but the shooting scotched that possibility. The Arrans had been followed from the Carilon . . .

He shook his head, to the barber's annoyance.

'Sorry,' he apologised. To himself: 'That won't do. I followed 'em, and there was nothing else on their tail. So—the thief must have been waiting in Lord's Avenue. So the house where Tim and Toby called was watched. The watcher was the swarthy man. He stole papers to see who the Arrans were and why they were calling at the house. Thereafter the arrest; and the shooting followed. The two things that matter are: who shot the thief, and who are the Arrans visiting?'

He did not take long to find an answer.

'The sister of Carris, of course. They were going to tell her about Nick's death, and I believe 'em, even if they did get a funny letter-heading. So on that theory, the girl's being watched.'

'A little more off the top, sir?'

Burke surveyed himself in the mirror, saw the clock reflected in it, and found that he had been sitting there for just over ten minutes. He needed at least twenty for the fuss outside to subside.

'No,' he said, 'but I'll have a shampoo.'

'Very good, sir.'

Burke's only conscious thought for the next ten minutes was that he was a fool. No man can think while his head is being doused, lather is spitting and hissing above him, lean fingers are rubbing his scalp. But it ended at last.

'Thanks,' said Burke. He was smiling as he left the shop, and saw the traffic in the Marylebone Road going on much as usual. The taxi was still waiting, and the Arrans' car was there.

He saw the Arrans come out of the house, two men who, at that distance, looked very much alike. They stepped into the Frazer Nash, the engine hummed, and the car moved off.

The cabby was looking across the road at Burke.

Burke waved his hand towards the Frazer Nash. The cabby understood him, revved his engine and turned in pursuit. Wherever the Arrans were going they would be pursued. For his part, Burke was going to watch the house.

It was safe enough to assume that the Arrans had heard nothing of the shooting affair, but Burke was puzzled. They should have been informed. Not until later did Burke know that the policeman had been struck by a bullet and had been unconscious for several hours.

Burke stood with his back to the hairdresser's window and rubbed his chin.

A different man from James William Burke might have

been bewildered by the events, and have been unable to shape any kind of reason out of them. But Burke was essentially solid and logical. He reasoned that the house where the Arrans had called sheltered Nick Carris's sister, and that she had been watched by the same people who had engineered that shooting. The Arrans had stayed so long that it was safe to assume they had seen the girl. She was, then, still there. And it was more than likely that she was still being watched by her sharpshooting friends.

So Burke decided to watch, in turn.

There was one thing he was anxious to do, however, and that was to confirm that someone named Carris did live in Lord's Avenue. A glance along the road showed him a post office within twenty yards, and where there was a post office there would also be a directory. It would take him little more than a couple of minutes to borrow the directory, and confirm part of his theory. Two minutes were worth risking.

He hurried to the post office, found it almost deserted, and the telephone booth empty. The A to D telephone directory told him that there were some fifty people named Carris on the list of subscribers. Fifty . . .

Carris, Arthur . . .

Carris, Augustus . . .

Carris, B. A. . . .

'Got it!' muttered Burke, as he traced his forefinger downwards. 'Carris, N. C., 17, Lord's Avenue.'

He replaced the directory and hurried out. Lord's Avenue was deserted and Burke was conscious of a little pleasing satisfaction at his own perspicacity. And then he had a shock.

A closed Daimler car swung out of the Marylebone Road, and stopped outside Number 17, Lord's Avenue.

A Daimler saloon.

3

BURKE PAYS A VISIT

B urke's fists were clenched. There was a little glitter in his eyes and, inconsequently, piety in his heart.

'Save me,' he murmured very softly, 'from putting a foot in the wrong place.'

As he watched the Daimler he pulled his wallet from his pocket. A glance told him that he had ten or twelve pounds, enough for likely emergency.

He watched a fat man climbing from the Daimler, a fat man in a chauffeur's uniform. A second man followed, lean, well-dressed, and approaching middle-age. He stepped lithely enough and hurried to Number 17. Burke heard the rat-tat on the door.

Burke lifted a hand towards a passing cabby at the same time, and beckoned the man as he stopped his cab.

As he approached, Burke dipped into his pocket, brought out three half-crowns, and passed them. The cabby's eyes widened.

Burke didn't look at him, but watched Number 17.

'Get to a telephone,' he said, 'and call Piccadilly 17851.

That's a garage. Tell 'em to send the fastest small car they've got to this place. Opposite Number so-and-so Marylebone Road. Then pull your cab up, with the flag down, and wait for me. If I want you, I'll call, if I don't you're in pocket.'

'What name shall I give the garage, sir?'

'Burke. Spelt with a U and an E.'

The cabby went on his way. Burke had seen the lean man enter Number 17, Lord's Avenue, and noticed the chauffeur standing by the Daimler, which suggested he didn't expect to wait long. At a rough estimate, it would take a quarter of an hour for the car from the garage to get to that spot, after the telephone message had been delivered.

'So if he's out in less than twenty minutes,' thought Burke, 'I'll have to use the cab. Damn all, why do I get these blasted hunches?'

He was being ungrateful to the sixth sense that guided him; he was backing a hunch that when the lean man came from the house he would be accompanied by a girl, and he told himself that, if she did come, his task was to follow her.

'So that's that!' he muttered, five minutes later. 'Here she comes.'

He was unable to get a good view of the girl whom he imagined to be Nick Carris's sister. But she was slim and straight, dressed in a becoming suit of navy blue, and gave him an impression of capability. She was walking hurriedly next to the lean, middle-aged man, towards the Daimler. The plump chauffeur held the door open and the couple disappeared.

'They're sending at once,' said the cabby, arriving at that moment.

'They'll be too late,' said Burke, briskly. 'Get into Lord's Avenue, and keep on the Daimler's tail. Save us,' he added for his own benefit, 'from a run in the country.'

He jumped into the cab and looked back through the

window. As far as he could see there was no one following. As the cab went along Lord's Avenue in the wake of the Daimler he kept his watch, but still nothing happened.

'That'll help,' he told himself, picking up the speaking tube. 'Sam, if you get a chance at a block, I'd like to draw level with the Daimler and look inside.'

The driver nodded. Burke leaned back in the cab and lit a cigarette. He felt an odd tangle of emotion inside him, partly exhilaration, at the things that had happened. He wondered, grimly, what had happened to the men who had been shot.

He would have been more than satisfied by the departure of the Arrans and the arrival of the Daimler. The shooting affair was an unwanted extra—and told him more than anything else could have done that this affair was something outsize. So far as he was concerned, the girl was the key at the moment.

The cabby tapped the window. Burke leaned forward to see the Daimler in front of him in a block. Carefully the cabby eased his taxi into a gap, and Burke looked inside.

He was safe in doing so. The chauffeur, the lean man and the girl, could see him a dozen times and not recognise him. It was a pleasant feeling that he was watching them without being suspected. He looked towards the girl. For a moment he could only see her hands, folded across her lap. The lean man was in the way, an aristocratic-looking gentleman with iron-grey hair. It was a striking face, regular in feature, very white and severe. Burke would have no difficulty in recognising it again.

'But it's the girl I want to see,' Burke murmured.

He had his wish a moment later, and his heart almost stopped. For the girl was leaning back against the cushions of the car, and her skin was deathly white against the grey upholstery. Her eyes were closed.

'This gets worse,' muttered Burke.

He was affected by the pale beauty, but was thinking of the pallor of her cheeks rather than her features. For he was ready to bet that she was drugged.

Then the Daimler moved forward, and the girl disappeared from Burke's sight. This was the one thing he had needed to fill him with savage hatred of the men who had committed murder and who, he told himself, had abducted the girl.

But if they *had* abducted her, how had they persuaded her to leave the house in Lord's Avenue? She had been conscious then, walking of her own free will.

For the next ten minutes there was a succession of traffic stops, forward dashes, blaring of horns and squealing of brakes. The Daimler's better acceleration was making the cabby's job a difficult one, but the man stuck to his task. The Daimler crossed the West End and made for the Victoria district.

'Not Sloane Square,' implored Burke, remembering the ins and outs of the streets between Victoria and Chelsea.

His prayer was answered. The Daimler hummed along King's Road, gathering speed with every yard. Only a set of traffic lights enabled the cab to keep in touch with its quarry.

'The open road,' Burke thought, grimly.

Just as they were flashing along New King's Road towards Putney, his fears were broken. The Daimler slowed down, turned left, and Burke recognised Hurlingham Polo Grounds. There were several large houses near there, standing in their own grounds. Would the Daimler stop by one of them?

Burke picked up the speaking tube.

'If it stops, drive past,' he said.

The driver nodded. Presently the Daimler pulled up outside one of the large houses, which did not, however, boast a drive. Burke saw the name, written on the closed fanlight.

He repeated it to himself several times, then said:

'Take the first turning, right or left, and stop as soon as you're out of sight.'

' 'Old tight,' said the cabby.

The cab swung round to the left, and Burke stumbled. He grinned ruefully and reminded himself that the cabby was earning his money. His fingers were on the handle of the door as the driver applied his brakes slowly, and the cab came to a standstill. He got out.

'You're doing fine,' he said, passing a pound note over. 'Turn your cab and wait in case I need you all of a sudden'.

'Don't want no 'elp, Boss, do you?'

'Sam,' said Burke, 'that was a kindly thing to say, the kindliest thing I've heard today. I might do. Do you know what a Tommy-gun is?'

The cabby's rugged face went still.

'Obviously you do,' said Burke. 'Well, a man in this Daimler used one a little while ago. So if there's a shindy and you've a wife and children, drive this as fast as it'll go, and don't look back. Things will not be healthy.'

But the cabby did not, apparently, think so fast.

'Machine-gun attack,' he muttered. 'I 'eard about that, mister. Wottaryer carrying?'

'I'm a peaceable man,' said Burke.

'I'll cover you,' said the cabby.

'I'm very glad I met you,' said Burke.

With a grin that made the cabby a friend for ever, he swung round and walked towards Longtree House. He was still marvelling on the nature of taxi drivers.

'Such a man,' murmured Burke, 'deserves much for his courage. Ump. The Daimler's still there.

28

So was the chauffeur, fat and stiff in his seat. Burke swung along, looking neither right nor left, but actually keeping Longtree House under surveillance. He was a hundred yards away, and had stopped to light a cigarette, when the door opened and the grey-haired man stepped towards the Daimler. Burke had hardly drawn at his cigarette when the Daimler purred past him. He caught a glimpse of driver and passenger, and realised he wasn't suspected.

If he had been, there would have been trouble. That part of Fulham is practically deserted during the week-day, and that afternoon was no exception. Murder could have been done, and, providing it was done silently, might have gone unnoticed for an hour or more.

The Daimler was safely away before Burke turned back towards Longtree House. What manner of people there were in that house was a complete mystery. It was even possible that the girl had gone there willingly, that the drug he had imagined was non-existent. But a sudden vision of her pallid face sent his doubts flying.

All the same, he felt uneasy about trying to force an entry into Longtree House. In the many games he had played in the past, he had always covered himself against emergency. Now he had no more safe support than the cabby. A warning reared up inside him.

It was in this moment of hesitation that he thought of Bob Carruthers.

He had known Carruthers for many years, and had last heard from him, two months before, from an address in Putney. Carruthers, claiming he was leading the healthy life, had taken one of the new flats facing Wimbledon Common. He could swing a fist with any man and he knew which end of a pistol ejected the bullet; more, he had no concern for his safety in a scrap.

'Let him be in,' murmured Burke, hurrying back to the cab driver. 'Sam, find the nearest phone, look up a man named Carruthers—C-a-r-r-u . . .'

'I know it,' said Sam.

'In a mansion flat on Putney Heath,' said Burke. 'If you get through to him in person, tell him to bring a gun. If you have to leave a message, just say he's wanted here, urgently. Tell him Burke.'

'Wiv a U and a Nee,' grinned Sam.

Burke smiled as the man swung into his seat. Then he waited at the corner, watching Longtree House, while keeping out of sight.

The waiting made him sweat. He saw, time and time again, the mental vision of the girl's dead-white face, and he hated to think that anything might happen to her while he was kicking his heels.

The cab hummed into sight at last, and the driver's face was sufficient indication of the success of his errand. As he drew up by Burke, he said:

' 'E's on 'is way, Boss, with,' the man's rugged face twisted in comical disgust, 'a battle-axe. So he says.'

'Believe less than half of what you hear,' grinned Burke joyously. 'How far is Putney Heath from here?'

'About three miles, Mister.'

'Ten minutes might bring him,' grunted Burke.

Just over ten minutes later, Bob Carruthers, driving an M.G. Sports, entered the road. He was dressed in silver greys, despite the bleak March day, his fair head was bared, his fair skin was aglow, and his methods with the wheel were murderous. He drew up, and most people would have expected a screeching of brakes. None came.

'Anything happened?' he asked, as he ran his car past the cab and pulled up.

'Not yet,' said Burke. 'There's no time for talking, Bob, but there's a girl in a house along here who doesn't want to be, I fancy.'

'*You* fancy?' Carruthers smiled knowingly.

'Keep your humour,' chided Burke, 'for people who might see something funny in it. Guns?'

'Gun.'

'It'll do,' said Burke. He turned to the cabby. 'Keep your eyes and ears open, and if we're not out of this place in half an hour, call the local police station. O.K.?'

'With me,' said Sam.

'What's it all about?' asked Carruthers, as the two men walked towards Longtree House.

'I don't know much about it, but I do know it starts with machine-guns, and the Lord knows where it might end. But the job is to get into that house.'

'There's a girl in there and you want to get her out?' observed Carruthers.

'Something,' Burke said drily, 'has improved you.'

They turned into the gate leading to Longtree House, hurried up the steps and knocked on the solid oak door. There was no sound for a moment. Burke knocked again. What would happen when the door opened? What chance had he of getting the girl out? What excuse could he offer if he found he had stumbled into a mare's-nest, if the girl had been brought from the Lord's Avenue house by relatives seeking to comfort her after the news of her brother's death? It was possible.

He stopped thinking, suddenly. The sound of footsteps came, and he saw Carruthers stiffen. There was a metallic click as a key turned. The door opened slowly.

An old man, so old that he looked feeble and exhausted with the sheer burden of life, stood blinking at them. His hooded eyes drooped; his nose was like parchment-covered bone. His face was bloodless, and his hands were all skin, bone and blue vein. He was dressed in black coat and trousers that sagged about his frail figure, and only the utmost tip of his toe-cap showed beneath his trousers.

He quavered:

'Yes—gentlemen?'

Burke put a foot against the door. The girl was in here; that much was certain. The thing was to make sure she was here against her will.

'I'd like to see Miss Carris,' he said.

In one way it was madness, of course. He had given away the fact that he knew she was here. It might easily lead to disaster if she was a prisoner; on the other hand, if she was with relatives it would be revealed very quickly.

'Car-ris.' The old man made it two separate words. 'I think you've made a mistake, gentlemen. No one here named Car-ris.'

Burke pushed his foot farther into the hall.

'You're old enough,' he said sadly, 'to tell the truth, Grandad. Do you mind if we come in?'

The old man's eyes flickered.

'Gentlemen . . .' All the dignified protest in the world was in that one word.

Burke took the frail arm and pushed the man back gently into the hall.

'We're not going to bite,' he said. 'We just don't believe you, and we're going to make sure.'

He stopped, with his fingers still on the old man's arm. Carruthers, at his side, grunted. Both of them were staring at the massive figure of a man standing halfway up a flight of stairs. There were points about the man's face that warranted attention, but at the moment they were concerned only with his right hand, and the blue-grey automatic in it.

'Let them in, Jasper,' said the man on the stairs. His voice was very smooth. 'Let them in, and we'll have a good look at them. They must be clever to have found us.' He grinned unpleasantly as Burke stepped forward. Burke saw a heavy face, red-skinned, heavy-jowled, with the purple traceries of drink in his cheeks and nose, and with two gold teeth behind thick lips. He saw, too, something vicious and cruel in a pair of bloodshot beady eyes. 'Well,' he went on, still softly. 'I suppose you've brought a message from Craigie, have you?'

He was searching their faces; what he saw disappointed him.

His suavity dropped from him, suddenly.

'Move!' he ordered. 'You'll find your tongues in a minute, or . . .'

Carruthers coughed, very gently.

'Have you ever heard,' he asked conversationally, 'of the practice of firing through your pocket?'

The words dropped like ice into the hall. There was a moment of utter silence. And then Burke heard two sharp zutts! Flames stabbed from the gun in the massive man's hand, but at the same instant the hand dropped, while the bullet from his gun stubbed into the staircase. Blood streamed from his fingers, profanity from his lips.

'Jim,' said Bob Carruthers. 'I don't like your friends.'

4

TWO ARE ADMITTED

Burke admitted, later that day, that if there had been anyone else in the house it might have been a different story. He accused himself of taking unnecessary chances, too, by breaking in with Carruthers as his only companion. Against that was the fact that the cabby had instructions to go to the police unless he returned in half an hour, and he *had* waited for Carruthers instead of going in by himself. But there was an element of luck in the raid on Longtree House that might not be present in later developments.

The old man was leaning against the door, gasping. The massive man was still standing on the stairs, fascinated by the sight of Carruthers's automatic, now out of that worthy's pocket.

Burke stepped forward, picked up the other automatic and pocketed it. Then:

'Where is she?' he demanded.

'She's all right,' the man gasped. 'I'll get her.'

'You'll lead the way,' grunted Burke. 'What do you call yourself?'

'I'm Hermann, Gustav Hermann.'

'How many others are there here?'

'None at all!'

'For every one we find,' said Burke grimly, 'we'll put a bullet through your thick hide, and the last one will be fatal.'

'But there's no one here,' Hermann was gulping hard. 'Just Jasper and me and the girl.'

'That'll be just as well,' said Burke.

He expected to find that Hermann was speaking the truth, and was vindicated. The house was smaller than it looked from outside, with eight large rooms, and two smaller ones, upstairs. In one of these, stretched out on a bed and still unconscious, they found the girl. She was breathing evenly, and so far as they could see was not hurt.

Burke grunted.

'Take her down to the cab, Bob.'

Carruthers frowned.

'Why the cab? What's the matter with my ... ?'

'Brain?' asked Burke gently. 'Bob, your bus is a beautiful bus, but it's an open one. The cab's closed.'

'Hmm,' said Carruthers. 'I'll let you get away with it. What are you going to do?'

'Wait until you come back, and then have a look round. The cabby will look after the girl.'

Carruthers lifted the girl gently from the bed, and carried her downstairs, wondering why Burke had not taken her himself; and Burke was wondering, wryly, the same thing.

Hermann was standing by the wall, his face the colour of putty. From the moment the tables had been turned, he had lost every semblance of courage. It was strange, Burke thought, that a gang which was able to organise machine-gun raids and abductions should employ a craven-hearted specimen like this. In many ways it was better Hermann was

35

yellow; he would talk more easily, and Burke wanted to hear him talk.

'Having started with names,' he said, as he heard Carruthers walking across the hall below, 'we might as well carry on with names. The fat boy in uniform.'

Hermann licked his lips.

'That's Dowson,' he muttered. 'Fat Dowson.'

'I know he's fat,' said Burke. 'What does his boss call himself? The tall, lean one with a face like an archbishop?'

Hermann licked his lips again, but this time he said nothing. Burke knew the man was scared. He waited a moment, smoothing the barrel of Hermann's automatic, and then:

'You seem to have an idea,' he said evenly, 'that I'm soft-hearted. I'm not. If I ever had been, my heart would have been turned to stone by one glance at you. Gus—the name of your boss.'

Hermann looked to and fro, desperately. He moved his feet, one across the other, and his hands were twitching against his trousers.

'A stomach wound,' said Burke, 'is painful, and you take a long time dying.'

Hermann stared into a pair of grey eyes that were merciless.

'When I say three . . .' began Burke.

Then he stopped.

Hermann's eyes shifted for a moment towards the door. There was no one there, but the sound of a powerful car engine floated upwards, and there was a noise of brakes. Burke guessed why Hermann had stalled. He had been expecting fresh arrivals.

'This will do,' snapped Burke, 'for the time being.'

He stepped swiftly across the room before Hermann

realised he had moved. A fist that had knocked men unconscious took Hermann beneath the point. The man's head went
back and he staggered, arms waving upwards. His chin jutted
out nicely, and Burke's second blow sent him thudding against
the wall. Burke didn't wait to see him slump down. He walked
to the door and into the passage. As he reached the landing he
saw three men enter the front hall and heard the quavering
voice of the ancient Jasper.

'There's one of them upstairs.'

A red-faced man swore. Another lantern-jawed tough spat
on the floor and dropped his hand towards his pocket. The
third man snapped:

'Who is it?'

'By the grace of God,' said Burke from the landing, 'James
William Burke, now and for ever at your service. Keep your
hand very still, because my gun's in my hand and I'm aching to
use it.'

The three men stared upwards, their eyes on the gun.
Burke sauntered down the stairs, telling himself that he was
looking at a bunch of the toughest gentry it had been his priv-
ilege to meet. There was, in the eyes of the three men, the cold
expressionlessness that denotes the killer.

The lantern-jawed man moved his hand swiftly, thinking
Burke unsighted. Flame stabbed from the big man's gun, and
the lantern-jawed one gasped and clutched his wrist.

'I warned you,' said Burke. 'Get right against the wall. A
yard away from each other, that's right. Stay there until I'm
gone. Don't move too quickly afterwards, unless you want to
get a puncture like Sonny's.'

He veered round as he passed them, keeping them under
range all the time. He moved casually enough, and not one of
them dared take another chance. There was something grim

about Jim Burke as he watched the gauntlet of their eyes, and measured each one in his mind for future reference. He had achieved the main object of his visit, by getting the girl away. Other things would follow soon, but for the time being the watchword was 'getaway'.

He stepped back on to the porch and waved a hand to catch the attention of the cabby or Carruthers. It was Carruthers who came, his right hand in his pocket.

'This gentleman also has a gun,' said Burke to the trio. To Carruthers: 'Hold 'em while I bring your car round, Bob. You can jump in as I'm passing.'

Carruthers kept the men lined up inside the house while Burke went for the M.G., and told the cabby to get away at once with the girl. 'Seventeen Lord's Avenue,' he said. 'Where we came from. Wait there for me.'

The man let in his clutch and grinned.

'If you arsks me,' he said, 'I reckon yer a ruddy marvel, mister.'

'Whenever I'm suffering from an inferiority complex,' said Burke cheerfully, 'I'll certainly ask you, Sam. If you lose that girl you'll lose your head.'

He watched the cab turn the corner, then hopped into the M.G., revved the engine and took the car round towards Longtree House. He stopped outside the open door as Carruthers backed towards him. Not until the trio was out of sight did Carruthers put his gun away. And then he rubbed his hand down the back of his head.

'What a waste of bullets,' he said.

'What's a waste of bullets?' demanded Burke.

'The five in my gun,' mourned Carruthers. 'You've got a nerve. Supposing that bunch had been there when we called?'

Burke negotiated a corner.

'Supposing we'd found 'em?' he said. 'There wouldn't have been a waste of bullets. Pity, wasn't it?'

'Hmm,' said Carruthers obscurely.

Craigie was stuffing the bowl of his meerschaum as he regarded the Arran twins. He was worried, because:

'When that wounded policeman recovered consciousness,' he said, 'he reported that he'd arrested the man on the accusation of another man who'd seen a theft from a car in Lord's Avenue. Yours was the only car in the avenue then, while the dead thief had papers from your dashboard in his pockets. So the shooting was connected with your visit to Miss Carris.'

'And she's gone out,' grunted Timothy.

'And hasn't been seen for three hours,' added Craigie. 'Well, there's nothing for it but to keep watching.'

'What about the Krotz angle?' asked Toby.

'I haven't decided what to do,' said Craigie. 'If there's an English connection, I'll want you over here. If there's not, you'll probably have a European trip, and it won't be a pleasant one.'

'Nor was the last,' said Toby, grimly.

He left Whitehall, with Timothy, and drove to their Auveley Street flat. The sight of a red M.G. outside did not surprise them. They were thoughtful and, like Craigie, worried. The death of an agent was a common enough thing; the use of vitriol as a means of torture was not. It wasn't until they opened the door of their flat that they realised the M.G. outside meant visitors for them. Past the solemn figure of Jeans, their general factotum, they saw the yellow hair of Bob Carruthers, and Burke's face.

'Well . . .' began Timothy.

'Well,' said Burke, 'but it's hackneyed. Had a nice ride, chaps?'

Toby regarded him with disfavour.

'I never did like you,' he said.

'Pity,' said Burke. 'Things have been happening, Tim and Tobias. A certain lady . . .'

The twins went very still. For a moment no one spoke, but Burke was smiling grimly. At last:

'What do you know about it?' asked Toby.

'Lots,' said Burke. 'I was curious and followed you from the Carilon. I saw you go into the Carrises' house, saw a man take some papers from your car, reported it to an intelligent Robert, saw the shooting, guessed it wasn't a picnic, waited for you to leave Miss Carris . . .'

'Breathe,' murmured Carruthers.

Burke paused.

'And later,' he continued, 'I saw her leave the house, didn't like the look of it, followed her out to a place in Hurlingham, sent for Bob, took the girl out of the lion's den, talked to Gus, and . . .'

'Damn it,' gasped Toby, taken aback for once in his life, 'you're joking, Jim.'

'You can't play billiards,' said Burke sorrowfully, 'and you're slow on the uptake.'

'And Pat's all right?' demanded Timothy incredulously.

'If Pat's Miss Carris, yes.'

'Thank the Lord for that!' said Timothy. 'Now let's have it, Jim—start to finish.'

'Half a mo',' said Toby. He walked to the door, opened it, bellowed for Jeans and demanded tea. Jeans, to the astonishment of the Arrans and the approval of the visitors, had already prepared it.

'That shows you,' said Timothy virtuously, 'what nice harmless tastes we have.'

'Shut,' said Carruthers.

'Shut what?' asked Timothy, blindly.

'Pubs are,' said Carruthers.

The resultant outbreak worked itself out, and Burke told his story. There was a silence after, that could almost be felt.

'There's something on,' Burke said. 'I'm in it, so is Bob. I think we've earned a bigger share.'

The twins exchanged glances.

'Half a mo',' said Toby again. He left the room, and from the passage came the ting of a telephone as the receiver was taken off its hook. Three men smoked and the fourth talked rapidly into the telephone. The ting came again. Toby came back, solemn-faced.

'You're going to be admitted,' he said. 'But you'll have to come to Whitehall, first. I needn't say,' he added awkwardly, 'that once you're in this, you can't drop out.'

'And so,' Gordon Craigie said, an hour later, 'I can use both of you. I know enough about you to be sure you're safe. But you'd better know that the chances are fifty-fifty on getting killed.'

'Hmm,' said Burke. 'I'm hardly surprised.'

'He'd have been dead,' said Carruthers blandly, 'but for me.'

Craigie's lips drooped in a smile, and he reached for his meerschaum.

'You've helped already, more than you can guess,' he said, stuffing the bowl. 'I didn't know there was an English side to this affair, but I do now. It's obvious that Miss Carris was abducted just so that your archbishop, Burke, could find out what story she had been told about Carris's death. They wanted to find out, from her, whether he had managed to get back to England. They'll know, now, that he did, for they'll be convinced you two men were agents of the Department. So . . .' Craigie's fingers were steady as he struck a match. 'I want to tell you something about a man named Krotz.'

5

HISTORY OF A LATHIAN
GENTELMAN

Most people know that during the years of nineteen-fourteen and nineteen-eighteen there was fought a war to end war. Most people know, also, that after gathering at Versailles certain statesmen and diplomats decided that, to ensure the ending of war, a number of mid-European countries should be cut into small pieces. Some of these pieces were stuck, literally, on to other and larger pieces, some were given to countries that had not been vivisected, and others—this was perhaps the crowning brilliance of the arrangement—were given 'independence' and told to manage their own affairs. This left a Europe made up of a number of small, independent states which were united by blood and countless centuries as one, but with their unity no longer acknowledged, and with a number of large states with a central government endeavouring to rule a country comprising people of half a dozen mixed nationalities. If those nationalities had bred quiet, undemonstrative peoples all might have been well, but patriotism was very fierce and it was no uncommon thing to one newly made nation split into four or five separate enthusiasms, united in nothing but lines on the map and a hatred of the ruling government—which was, of necessity, hybrid.

One of the smallest countries was Lathia.

Lathia has a long coastline on the Baltic, with one important port, Rikka. It is bordered on the north by three smaller—and comparatively peaceful—states, on the east by the Republic of Russia, and on the south partly by Poland and partly by Germany. Its chief industries are coalmining, iron-smelting and timber-growing, and it is unique in as far as its people, made up of half a dozen different nationalities, are sufficiently satisfied with their lot to desire no reversion to their original status. Certain statesmen claim, from time to time, that Lathia is proof positive of the success of the treaties aforementioned.

Certainly it is true that Lathia, since the early twenties, has been too busy to worry about internal strife. In a measure, that may explain the position of Marius Krotz.

He was born of Eurasian peasants. History records that his early days revealed his cleverness and his cruelty. He became a revolutionist for as long as he gained profit from stirring up trouble in European countries.

Then Marius Krotz became a revolutionary with a difference. He advocated that old friend of the Powers, peaceful penetration. The fire seemed to have disappeared from his tongue; he was tolerated in erstwhile hostile countries, and became almost the pet of the Lathian Government which allowed him to sit in the House as representative of a small, hot-headed constituency in the suburbs of Rikka, the Lathian capital as well as its chief port.

But if the Lathian Government was convinced of the harmlessness of Marius Krotz, other governments were not. France, Great Britain and Italy in particular watched him through their various agencies—in the case of England through the Department called Z.

From 1925, then, until 1928, Krotz did nothing to attract attention. It was a fact that he lived in luxurious style outside Rikka, in a villa that so closely resembled a palace that certain emissaries of the Soviet felt thoroughly at home within its walls. One thing reported regularly to the office in Whitehall was the friendliness of Krotz and the Russians, but he was not the only ex-firebrand who interested the Soviet republic, and there was nothing abnormal about the association.

Gordon Craigie might have wondered where the revolutionary, who had been kicked out of nearly every country in Europe a few years before, obtained his money—for his wealth was legendary—but for knowledge of the huge payment he had received for the unsuccessful attempt to start a revolution in Denmark. This made it reasonable to assume that Krotz received other, regular payments to keep him quiet.

It might be wondered why, if Marius Krotz was reckoned powerful enough to cause grave trouble in Lathia or any other country, he was not quietly assassinated. There were two strong reasons. One, he had a large following, and the cost of repressing any trouble that might arise from his murder would probably exceed the cost of paying him to live quietly. Two, he never travelled alone, and the villa on the heights outside Rikka was like a fortress.

It should, perhaps, have been mentioned before that Lathia was—and is—a kingdom, with a king who was no more than a puppet for his ministers. The Secret Service agents of the various big Powers who had the friendship of King Ferdo's ministers might be blamed for failing to watch him more closely, knowing the ease with which his bodyguard could be bribed. Reproaches of any kind were useless, however, after King Ferdo went for a short sea-trip in the May of 1929, and came back a corpse. It was said that he fell overboard during a squall.

Now it is necessary to glimpse the royal differences in Lathia. If the country itself and its peoples had a kind of Nordic caim, the royal household was bitter, fractious and petty. Ferdo's throne was clamoured for by his two brothers—the king had been a bachelor—Frederik and Klaus. Klaus was the strong man, knowing his own mind, capable of governing for himself and of setting up a dictatorship. He was, moreover, fair-minded and conscious of his duty to his country. Frederik, two years older than Klaus, wanted nothing more than perpetual change in his amusements and mistresses.

Klaus had the support of the Government; Frederik was due for kingship by reason of his seniority. But the royal house of Lathia had never been taken too seriously by its government, and three months after Ferdo's death, Klaus was made king, after signing an agreement to keep the country in constitutional hands. Lathia became the good boy of Europe, and European diplomats patted themselves on the back.

It can be imagined that Frederik did not take kindly to this. He sulked, threatened violence and became so difficult in his pleasures that it was necessary to import several beauties from other countries. He might have been satisfied, then, but for . . .

Krotz.

Krotz had been behaving himself for so long that it was not suspected he was still the firebrand revolutionary with an eye on his own fortune. Still less was it suspected that he had the ear of the Left party in the Lathian Government.

The revolution was as near bloodless as any revolution can be. King Klaus was shot, his personal bodyguard bribed to swear it had been suicide, and Frederik was crowned. Lathia woke up one morning to learn this, and, in effect, turned over, yawned, and went back to sleep.

But Frederik was king and Krotz was his right-hand man.

The Secret Service men in Lathia watched the new regime carefully, but the house seemed in order. Krotz was the power behind the throne, but was using his power well. Lathia was still the good boy of Europe, and statesmen who had been worried lest their treaties should be torn up by the last loyal adherent heaved audible sighs of relief.

Such was Lathia.

'Of course,' said Gordon Craigie, as he reached the end of the story, 'we've been watching Krotz very carefully. The man is dangerous and unscrupulous. We knew that before Nick Carris discovered it. But Nick didn't discover what game he's playing, and we've got to.'

Craigie stopped, tapped out his meerschaum and started to refill it. The Arran twins grunted, fair-headed Carruthers proffered cigarettes, and Jim Burke said:

'You could name a dozen men in Europe who've had much the same history.'

Craigie nodded.

'So what makes you think he's playing anything more than a personal game?' asked Burke.

Craigie smiled a little and rubbed his chin.

'You'll find that we suspect everyone until we know he is innocent,' he said. 'We have to. But there are circumstances that make Krotz obviously a danger—aren't there?'

'You mean,' Burke said, 'that Krotz was obviously anxious to find whether Carris had arrived in England with some specific news. Therefore Krotz is doing something that makes him afraid of the interest of—what do you call your-selves? the Secret Service?—and it follows that the Service

wouldn't be worried about a purely national—Lathian—
stunt. Is that it?'

Craigie nodded.

'That's just it,' he agreed.

Burke laboured the point.

'So Krotz is playing a game that might have international
complications?'

'I should say definitely yes.'

'What happens,' demanded Burke, 'if you just blot Krotz
out?'

'You mean if he dies?' asked Craigie gently.

'Er—accidentally, of course.' Burke smiled. 'He sounds
poisonous enough to deserve it, so there can't be any
conscience scruples.'

'Take a hypothesis,' said Craigie. 'Assume you saw a card-
board box and wanted to see what was in it. You wouldn't
pitch it in the fire and destroy it, would you?'

'No,' said Burke. 'Before you lose Krotz, he must talk.' He
paused and eyed Craigie thoughtfully. Craigie said nothing,
for he was impressed by the potential of Jim Burke, and
wanted to get a further insight into the mind of the big man
who spoke very little, but usually to the point. 'And assuming,'
went on Burke, 'Krotz is running a political game, and not a
personal one, the fact that he's carrying a London agency
means it's got some connection with England.'

'Yes.' Craigie was satisfied that Burke was as shrewd as he
looked.

'They were the toughest bunch I've ever struck,' said the
big man, appreciatively. 'Gus Hermann's yellow, but the others
are the real gunman boys. And then there's the Archbishop. By
the way,' he added, quickly, 'how many men have you got
watching Longtree House?'

Craigie smiled. It said much for Burke's respect for the

organisation into which he had just been admitted that he took it for granted Longtree House was watched from the moment Craigie had learned of it from the Arrans, by telephone.

'Three,' he said. 'If there's a move from there, we shall know.'

'What do you want us to do?' Burke asked.

'Go back to your flat and wait,' said Craigie. 'I'll send for you or write on that letter-heading.'

Burke grinned as he took a piece of paper adorned with the name of a prominent London business concern. On such paper the Arrans had received news of Nick Carris's death. On that particular piece of paper was a cypher.

'Learn it off by heart,' said Craigie, 'and burn it. One will do for both of you.'

Ten minutes later the four men left Department Z, by different routes, and Gordon Craigie sat back in his chair and chuckled. There was something devastating about Jim Burke. The affair at Hurlingham, it was true, had been fortunate in more ways than one, but Burke had handled that emergency in masterly fashion. He was likely to prove one of the most valuable agents Department Z had had for a long time.

Burke—and Marius Krotz.

Craigie remembered the burning eyes of Nick Carris, in that red, burned face, and he felt cold. If Krotz was capable of that . . .

The telephone on the desk burred out. Craigie stood up and walked to it.

Burke's deep voice came over the wire.

'Didn't know how much I ought to say, with the others there,' he said, and Craigie could imagine his eyes were creased at the corners. 'But there are one or two little things I'd like to know.'

'Such as?' asked Craigie.

'Can you make it easy for me to get a firearm licence?'

'Yes. Ask for Superintendent Miller, at the Yard, in an hour's time.'

'Thanks. Did Carris give you any message? Any idea of what's happening?'

'Nothing—only to watch Krotz.'

'Hmm. Am I a free agent?'

'Meaning?'

'Must I wait for things to happen, or can I root round a bit on my own?'

Craigie made a decision that he wouldn't have made with nine out of ten new agents.

'Do what you like, Burke, but be careful.'

'Thanks. I always am! By the way, is the Lathian language a teaser?'

'I've never tried,' said Craigie.

'Then,' said Burke, 'I'll tell you all about it in a week's time. If I need help and can't get in touch with you, what happens?'

'Call on Miller, at the Yard.'

'Thanks,' said Burke, appreciatively.

The line went dead. Craigie played thoughtfully with the receiver for a moment, then called the Chief Commissioner, Sir William Fellowes, a stony-faced gentleman with a slight limp.

It was frequently necessary for Craigie to get the help of Scotland Yard, but never had he been helped so willingly as during the term of Fellowes' office. Both men had a disrespect for the law that Fellowes enforced. If common sense told them that the law should be broken, it was at least bent.

'All right,' said Fellowes, as Craigie finished. 'I'll tell Miller to get things ready for Burke. Isn't that the big man who doesn't talk?'

'That sounds like him,' smiled Craigie. 'Do you know him?'

'Slightly,' said Fellowes.

'Get me everything you can on Burke—it's safest—and on Carruthers,' Craigie asked.

'History from their birth up,' said Fellowes. He hesitated. 'Have you told them much?'

'Not much more than they found for themselves,' said Craigie, grimly. 'Carruthers lives at Heath Mansions, Putney Heath. You know Burke's address?'

Fellowes said that he did, and the conversation finished. The Commissioner sent for Superintendent Horace Miller immediately, and told himself that Craigie rarely used a man whose credentials hadn't been fully tested. There must be something unusually convincing about Jim Burke.

After leaving Department Z, Burke had lost Carruthers and the Arrans, and had called Craigie from a nearby telephone kiosk. He was within five minutes' walk of Scotland Yard, and wanted to get that firearms licence. He had a cup of tea and a sandwich at a nearby café and, just over half an hour after he had spoken with Craigie, walked up the steps to Scotland Yard.

A bare-headed sergeant greeted him in the hall.

'Good afternoon, sir.'

'I'd like to see Superintendent Miller, please,' said Jim Burke.

'The sort,' thought the sergeant, 'who doesn't have to be kept waiting.' Aloud: 'Very good, sir.'

Superintendent Horace Miller proved to be a large, burly man, with sandy hair and milky skin, as if he had been dusted with flour that had spread all over him, clothes, face and hands. He had a pair of bushy brows that revealed shrewd blue eyes, and features that were rough-cut in a face that could only be labelled 'strong'. His dress was careless but comfortable, and he had a rather pleasant voice.

The two men eyed each other as Burke entered the Super's small office, and formed impressions. Both were favourable. Miller held out a large but well-shaped hand, and both grips were firm.

'I've heard you would be here,' said Miller. 'The licence will be along in a few minutes, Mr. Burke.'

'Just Burke,' said the big man.

Miller's earlier impression was strengthened.

'Pretty quick work,' added Burke.

'Even the police can hurry,' grinned Miller. 'It's not the usual procedure, of course, but in the circumstances . . .'

A round-faced sergeant entered, carrying the licence. Burke signed and paid for it, and the sergeant went out.

'I don't know what you're doing,' said Miller, 'but here's luck. Any time you're stuck, don't be afraid to call me.'

'Thanks,' said Burke. He created the impression that he was thinking hard. 'Longtree House, Super . . .'

'We had a call through about it earlier this afternoon,' Miller said. 'Owned by a man named Karen . . .'

'K?'

'K-a-r-e-n. Nothing known against him.'

'Any photographs available?' asked Burke.

'We're trying to get one or two,' Miller said.

'I'll phone you tomorrow,' said Burke. 'I'd like to know that gentleman. Karen isn't an English name.'

'He's a naturalised Englishman. Originally a Pole.'

'Ah,' said Burke. 'Then you'll have some information about him. How long has he been naturalised?'

'Just over a year. We've sent for his papers,' Miller added, 'and if you care to wait you can see them with me. Will you?'

Burke nodded.

'But carry on as if I'm not here,' he said.

In the next ten minutes Miller learned something about Burke that came to all his acquaintances in time. Burke kept absolutely still, without shuffling or moving. He possessed the ability to concentrate to a degree that was almost unnerving.

The messenger came, eventually, with the naturalisation papers. Adolf Karen had been born in Poland, of a Polish father and a Lithuanian mother. He was the director of a steel goods firm, bearing the suitable title of 'Smethwick, Karen and Company, Limited', and, prior to his naturalisation, he had been periodically in England for the Lathian branch of Smethwick and Karen, some of whose smelting works were in Lathia.

Burke noted these essentials, thanked Miller and left the Yard.

Did that information help Burke? Miller wondered, when he'd left.

It did, of course, for Mr. Adolf Karen's Lathian connection was very interesting. But Burke did not know how much Miller could be told.

He set himself, with some reluctance, to visit 17, Lord's Avenue, and Miss Patricia Carris.

6

BURKE HAS AN IDEA

J im Burke saw that Patricia Carris had blue eyes of a
directness and charm which sent the idea which had been
born, a few minutes before, out of his mind with a click.
The idea concerned the weedy-looking individual who had
been watching 17, Lord's Avenue. He might be a policeman, or
even a Department agent, Burke knew, but he had his doubts.

Doubts, ideas, and everything else went out, however, as
Burke looked into Patricia Carris's eyes, and saw the shadows
in them. It had been a guiding rule in Burke's life to put
anything right that he saw was wrong.

He had been admitted by a worried-looking servant and
kept waiting in the hall before being allowed to enter the
room facing Lord's Avenue, where Patricia Carris waited. He
had a confused idea that she was good to look at, and a fixed
idea that her eyes were the bluest he had ever seen.

Her voice was low-pitched; husky.

'I don't think I know you, Mr. Burke.'

Burke felt suddenly that here was a time when it was

useless to say little; he had to talk well enough to convince Patricia Carris that he was there with good intentions.

It occurred to him, vividly, that he had followed her to Hurlingham and taken her from the nastiest bunch of ruffians he had met and that, in those circumstances, it was absurd that she hadn't seen him before.

'Please sit down,' said Patricia.

Burke dropped into an easy chair, and the girl sat opposite him. Burke marshalled his thoughts.

'You know, don't you,' he said, 'that you went to Hurlingham?'

'Yes.' Patricia's hesitation was due in part to surprise, and in part to alarm.

'Good,' said Burke, 'that helps. I followed you there. Had a bit of a tussle getting you out.'

Patricia smiled quickly, breathlessly.

'So it was you!'

Burke nodded and fumbled for cigarettes.

'No, not for me,' said Patricia. 'I don't know how to thank you.'

'No, not a bit, don't worry about it,' said Burke, and his alarm seemed real. 'Glad I happened along in time to be useful. But I wonder if you'd mind telling me what happened, Miss Carris. Give me a general idea, so to speak.'

'From when?' Patricia Carris, for a girl who had been drugged a few hours before, was very self-possessed.

'From the time the Arrans left.'

If the shadow in her eyes were deeper, it did not affect the steadiness of Patricia's voice.

'You know, of course, that they brought me news of my brother's death?'

'Yes.'

'I just felt dead, for a little while,' Patricia said quietly. 'I'd hardly had time to realise it before the other man came. He claimed to be a solicitor with an urgent message concerning Nick. I didn't hesitate when he asked me to go with him to his office.'

'Naturally,' murmured Burke.

'But I hadn't been in the car more than a few minutes before he was threatening me with an automatic.' She smiled, a little wanly. 'I ought to explain that I'd accepted a cigarette from him, that explains how I was drugged. He asked me who had brought me the news of Nick's death. I didn't see any harm in telling him. Then he wanted to know whether they were close friends of the family, whether they had ever worked with Nick. Because I wouldn't answer, he showed his gun.'

'Hmm,' said Burke.

'I didn't think he could shoot me there,' said Patricia ingenuously, 'and if he wanted to know something I didn't think there was any danger. So I wouldn't speak.'

'Hmm,' said Burke again. He was thinking that Patricia Carris was worth her weight in gold. She had common sense, and she hadn't gone into hysterics at the sight of a gun.

'And then,' Patricia said, with a helpless little shrug, 'I went to sleep. The man—did you see him?'

'Yes.'

'Was very calm all the time. He didn't lose his temper when I wouldn't talk. Anyhow, that was the last I saw of him. I woke up in the back of a taxi, and the driver told me he'd brought me from Hurlingham on the instructions of a big man.'

'Nothing's happened since?'

'Nothing at all.'

'Any idea why the . . .' Burke wasn't thinking closely of his words. 'Bishop . . .'

'The *Bishop?*'

Burke grinned.

'Sorry. The johnnie who had the gun. I thought he looked like a cleric ought to be, and the name stuck. He was originally an archbishop. Any idea why he questioned you?'

'I haven't,' said Patricia, and went on quickly, 'but I know Nick often played a lot of dangerous games.'

'He told you about them?'

'No.' Patricia was very loyal to her brother. 'But he often disappeared for months at a time. And I guessed he'd been worrying the—bishop—who thought I might know something.'

Burke looked at her, squarely. 'You don't, of course?'

'No, I do not.'

'There's absolutely nothing you could have told him,' Burke persisted, 'that was reason enough to have made him collar you like he did?'

'Nothing at all,' said Patricia, and Burke felt a weight off his chest.

'Thank the Lord for that! I was half afraid you might be involved in this business, and it's likely to be noisy.'

'Tell me the truth,' said Patricia, very evenly. 'Nick was murdered, wasn't he?'

Jim Burke drew a deep breath.

'Yes,' he said.

'By the man with the gun?'

'No,' said Burke decisively. 'The man who shot him won't shoot anyone else.'

'But the same people,' Patricia insisted.

Burke shrugged his big shoulders.

'Yes. But he was liable to meet trouble, Miss Carris. He took risks and he died for something worth while. The Arrans will have told you that. Believe it, please.'

Patricia Carris said nothing for a moment, and there was an expression in her eyes that Burke didn't like. At last:

'He died for the same thing as you'll die for,' she said. 'And the Arrans. You'll go on and on until you take one risk too many, and then you'll die. *God!* It isn't fair.'

The quiet of the room seemed shattered. Patricia did not raise her voice, but the words rang out, and her lips quivered. Nick had been cut down in the fullness of his manhood, killed, *murdered,* and she hated the thing that had caused it.

Burke was strangely understanding.

'He died for peace,' he said, and there was a ring of sincerity in his voice.

Patricia looked at him. Her set face broke, suddenly, into a slowly widening smile. She nodded, and there was an expression in her eyes that made Burke's heart beat fast.

'For peace,' she echoed, very softly.

And then, unexpectedly, she turned her face away. Her hands went to her eyes and for the first time in his life Burke saw a woman crying without tears. He felt cold, and his muscles were set. There was nothing he could do.

Except get at Krotz.

The paroxysm was over at last. Patricia turned towards him again, and there was a smile on her lips which carried all the courage in the world.

'I'm sorry,' she said. 'You see, Nick was the only one of us left. But I'll be all right, now.'

Burke nodded and stood up.

'Are you staying here?'

'I think so.'

'I'd like to call,' he said.

'You'll be very welcome.'

'And if there's anything I can do . . .'

She nodded. There were tears in her eyes, now, Burke smiled at her, and his hand closed round hers. They held for a second, and then he turned away.

There is a frame of mind known briefly as feeling like the devil, and Jim Burke experienced it as he hurried out of the Lord's Avenue house towards his waiting taxi. But there was work to do, work not entirely that of avenging Nick Carris. He walked to the Post Office, after telling the cabby to go, and telephoned his Brook Street flat where, as he expected, Bob Carruthers was waiting for him.

'And I'd hoped,' said Carruthers bitterly, 'you'd been clouted over that thick skull of yours.'

'If you'd been missing for a couple of hours,' retorted Burke, 'I'd have known it. Are the twins there?'

'They're waiting at their flat.'

'Any message from anywhere?'

'Well,' said Carruthers sweetly, 'I didn't like to be inquisitive, so I told the little dears you'd be back later. One of 'em had a nice voice.'

'Supposing,' suggested Burke heavily, 'you tried not to be funny for a few minutes?'

'Your turn,' said Carruthers.

'Meet me at the Regal Cinema, in half an hour,' said Burke. 'If you see me and I don't notice you, keep waiting. That all right?'

'You haven't forgotten,' said Carruthers, 'that there might be a message from Craigie?'

'No, but I've a little spot of work for us. Half an hour, at the Regal.'

He closed down, and went out of the Post Office, lighting a cigarette, when he saw the weedy one talking to a thickset man dressed in navy blue and a bowler, the effect of which was set off to perfection by a pair of beautiful bright brown shoes. Burke started to walk, easily, towards Marble Arch and the Regal Cinema. Twice in as many minutes he almost cannoned into a passer-by, stepped aside and apologised and caught a glimpse of the man some twenty yards behind him.

Undoubtedly the man was a mug. Those brown shoes would have made him conspicuous anywhere, especially when there was a possibility that his shadowing would be spotted. But Burke felt kindly towards him for the muggishness; it helped considerably.

He stopped beneath a bus-stage notice, and hopped on to the first bus heading for Marble Arch. As he mounted the stairs he watched Brown Shoes' frantic efforts to catch the bus, and silently applauded as his trailer succeeded. At the nearest stopping-place to the Regal Cinema, Burke dropped off. Brown Shoes followed. Burke examined the photographs outside that magnificent hall of pleasure, jingled some coins in his pocket and finally booked a seat. He lounged in the foyer for some minutes, out of sight of the street, and was satisfied that Brown Shoes did not intend to follow him into the cinema.

He had little doubt, however, that his trailer would be watching and waiting outside. On that possibility he was staking heavily. He invariably worked on the assumption that he would win.

It was just twenty minutes past five when Carruthers entered the café where Burke was sitting. The fair-headed man's eyes roved the room, saw Burke but took no notice of him. Burke caught his friend's eye and beckoned.

'How'd she go?' asked Carruthers, dropping into a chair.

'Warmish,' said Burke.

'What's the game?'

'When I leave here,' said Burke, ordering tea for his friend, 'a stocky bloke in blue, bowler and brown shoes will come after me. I'm going to give him a run across London, and you're going to follow him following me.'

'Got it.'

'At'—Burke hesitated—'at seven o'clock, we'll be some-where in the suburbs. Wherever we are, do something to stop Brown Shoes following me. Just keep him busy for a couple of minutes. Then you follow *him* and I'll follow you. Clear?'

'Supposing he comes right back where he started from?' asked Carruthers, stirring his tea.

'We'll suppose that,' said Burke, 'when it happens.'

It was two minutes past seven on that bleak March evening when the man in the brown shoes, cursing the big man who had led him a pretty dance across London, tripped over the foot of a tall, cheery-looking gentleman with fair hair. Despite his profanity, the trailer had been congratulating himself. His outsized quarry was obviously trying to make sure he was not followed, but despite every effort, he, Brown Shoes, had kept on his tail. The price of this virtue, Brown Shoes decided, would be several pints of foamy stuff, and he hoped the big man didn't hang the hunt out too long. Thoughts of foamy stuff and praise of his own cleverness mingled with the man's determination not to lose his quarry, and the foot over which he stumbled came out of the blue.

He lurched forward, towards the hard pavement outside Walham Green Station. The fair-headed man shot out a saving arm.

'Whoa back! Lord, lad, I thought your napper had caught it that time. Sorry, can't say how sorry.'

If Brown Shoes was grateful for that saving arm he concealed it effectively. He swore.

'. . . clumsy . . .' he told Carruthers. 'Mind out of my way, you . . .'

Carruthers, whose right hand was gripping his shoulder, supposedly to save him, tightened his grip. The apologetic grin on his face disappeared.

'What was that?' he asked gently.

Brown Shoes tried to wrench his shoulder free. He was looking round desperately for the big man he had followed since five o'clock, and he caught a glimpse of that worthy disappearing into a taxi.

'If you don't drop yer ruddy arm,' he snorted, 'I'll . . .'

Carruthers gave a frosty grin.

'I shouldn't keep that up,' he advised. 'If you take that face and that language about with you often, you'll find the former's suffered because of the latter.' He tightened his fingers still more, and suddenly the grip was painful. 'Get me?'

Brown Shoes was in despair. The taxi was almost out of sight now.

'Listen, mate!' he implored, 'I've gotta train to catch. Never meant a thing, s'elp me.'

Carruthers relaxed his grip. Brown Shoes tore across the road, to try and catch a glimpse of the taxi with his quarry, but the cab was out of sight. Carruthers saw the man's thick lips forming words that were not listed in the *Oxford Dictionary*, and wondered what Burke was doing now.

After a few minutes' hesitation, Brown Shoes walked back to the station entrance. Carruthers hurried to the booking office, took a ticket to Barking, and walked on to the platform a few yards ahead of his quarry. It was a neat manœuvre, for Brown Shoes, seeing the fair-headed destroyer of his hopes on the platform ahead of him, would not dream of complications.

The ticket to Barking covered Carruthers for any part of London and Brown Shoes' suspicions were stifled before they were born.

At no time is Walham Green Station an inspiring place. Brown Shoes scowled ferociously at all and sundry, although he had not, apparently, seen Carruthers.

Then a tall, well-dressed man approached Brown Shoes, and, it seemed, asked for a match.

Now Bob Carruthers was a happy-go-lucky soul, and, as he saw Brown Shoes start up, look questioningly at the well-dressed man for a moment and then, in some confusion, search his pockets for a box of matches and in due course light the other's cigarette, he wondered whether everything was exactly what it seemed.

Was there a vague suggestion of kow-towing about the man in the natty, brown shoes and bowler? Did he look nervous, a little surprised and taken off his guard?

Carruthers thought he did. For the sixty seconds while the two men had murmured to each other and the courtesy of the cigarette-lighting had passed, Carruthers fancied Brown Shoes was standing as if before a superior. When the well-dressed man walked away, Brown Shoes was thoughtful and apparently happy. He was no longer scowling as if the world had done him wrong.

'Damn it,' murmured Carruthers, 'I wish Burke was here.'

True, Burke had said he would follow him; but the big man might not have had the opportunity.

The rumble of a distant train brought the half a dozen intending passengers towards the edge of the platform. Carruthers, his quarry and the well-dressed man were among them. The train came into sight, beneath the tunnel, the roaring and rumbling filling the station, there was a preliminary squeal of brakes . . .

Bob Carruthers heard, vaguely, a pounding down the steps leading from the booking hall to the platform, but he didn't turn to look. He was too interested in Brown Shoes, making sure he shared that worthy's carriage.

The train was twenty yards away.

A voice sounded in Carruthers' ear.

'Excuse me, sir . . .'

Carruthers turned—and the umbrella of the well-dressed man caught between his legs. He saw the gimlet blue eyes of the stranger, saw a suggestion of a smile on thin lips, and he knew it had happened intentionally.

But he was off his balance—and the train was fifteen yards away, roaring, rushing.

Carruthers pitched forward, his head towards the yawning rails. He saw the red belly of the oncoming train, heard the roaring, felt the hands of the well-dressed man touch him, apparently to help, actually to send him still further towards the hurtling death. Carruthers didn't think; he *felt* death!

He tried desperately, but couldn't steady himself. He was actually hanging over the edge of the platform. He knew what was happening, saw it mentally as he would see a slow-motion picture.

Someone shrieked!

A guard bellowed, a woman cried, the driver's face was twisted in alarm as he tried all he could to pull the train up in the five yards he had to spare.

Something caught at Carruthers' hand, stretched behind him in his great effort to pull back. His arm was jolted, a bone cracked, pain shot through him. He only knew that he was no longer falling downwards, he felt himself lifted into the air and then dropped on to the platform. The train rushed by. Somebody cried:

'Thank God!'
Carruthers grunted.

Jim Burke saw Carruthers ensnare Brown Shoes into an altercation outside Walham Green Station, stopped the taxi as it turned the first corner and paid an astonished driver five shillings. He hopped into the road and hid in a shop entrance while Brown Shoes tried to trace the taxi, failed, and walked back dispiritedly towards the station. Burke might have followed immediately, but there was the bare possibility that Brown Shoes wasn't alone. He saw the man whom he had called variously the Bishop, the Archbishop and things unprintable follow Carruthers and Brown Shoes into the station.

Burke booked his ticket to Whitechapel, and waited at the top of the stairs, watching Carruthers, Brown Shoes and the Bishop on the platform. Not until the train rumbled along did he realise what might happen. He saw the Bishop edging towards Carruthers, and he started down the stairs like a man possessed.

The passengers had the best view of the spectacle.

They saw a very big man with a face like granite hurtling towards a little bunch of waiting people, saw Carruthers trip over the well-dressed man's umbrella, felt the thrill of horror, saw Burke dashing through the little crowd, flinging men and women from his path, saw him make a desperate effort to reach Carruthers, catch that man's outflung hand and, taking the only chance of saving himself and Carruthers, fasten his grip and swing round. Carruthers was whirled in a half-circle before he was dropped. Burke went flying headlong against the wall of the station, saving himself by taking the full force of the fall on his hunched left shoulder.

He saw the little crowd surging towards him, and saw the face of the Bishop twisted into an expression that had little to do with episcopacy, the round startled eyes of the man with brown shoes almost starting from his head. Burke closed his eyes.

7

MR. KAREN PROTESTS HIS INNOCENCE

B urke opened his eyes again quickly, but he had needed that fraction of a second's rest from seeing or thinking. When the whirling in his head eased a little he looked round. The Bishop was standing at the edge of the crowd that had been swollen by half a dozen porters, a ticket-collector and a policeman. Brown Shoes, too, was on the edge of the crowd. A solicitous voice demanded:

'Take it easy, sir. Are you all right?'

Burke nodded.

'Lend me a hand,' he said, stretching his right arm upwards.

A porter gave him the necessary help, and he staggered to his feet, more winded and bemused than he thought, But agitating his fuddled mind was the fact that the Bishop was going to make a getaway.

'I'd like a word with the gentleman with the gamp,' said Burke. 'Yes—that one.'

A dozen pairs of eyes looked towards the Bishop, who might have made a break for safety had Burke not drawn attention to him. He stopped on the edge of the crowd and eyed Burke frostily.

'You want me, sir?'

'A word in your ear,' said Burke.

The Bishop stepped forward, reluctantly, and was immediately hemmed in. Burke looked at Carruthers who was staggering to his feet and feeling his shoulder tenderly. Someone said: 'Fetch a doctor.' Carruthers gritted his teeth and the pain eased.

'I'm all right,' he grunted, looking at Burke.

Burke nodded towards the train, and turned to the driver who was standing nearby. The man's expression might have been comical at another time. Relief transformed him.

Burke was feeling his real self, now.

'Better get going,' he said cheerfully. 'No damage done, driver.'

'I couldn't 'ave 'elped it, sir, did everything I could, b'lieve me.' The words came out with a rush. 'My, you didn't 'arf streak across.'

'No quicker than you jammed your brakes,' said Burke.

'Sure you're all right?' asked a guard.

'Both of us,' Burke assured him, with a glance at Carruthers, 'are fine. Let's get going, or you'll put the service out of gear. Er . . .' He looked at the Bishop, and only the Bishop saw the hardening of his eyes. 'Are you travelling on this train, sir?'

The other nodded. There was nothing else he could do.

'Then we can have our talk on it,' said Burke.

The sensation was over, the train had to complete its journey, the ticket-collector had deserted his post, and the policeman wasn't certain whether to report this as an accident or not. Burke convinced him that it wasn't necessary, and stepped into the nearest carriage, after the man whom he liked to call the Bishop, and a step in front of Brown Shoes. Carruthers brought up the rear. They sat down. The train started.

There was a moment's silence in the carriage, before Burke spoke.

'That,' he said grimly, 'was the neatest murder attempt I've seen for a long time, and the last one you'll be interested in —*Mr. Karen.*'

Karen!

The man with the benevolent face gasped. His eyes widened in alarm.

'My dear sir, you can't really mean . . .'

'Don't try to deny it,' snapped Burke. His face was very grim as he leaned back in his seat and surveyed the man he believed to be the ex-Polish owner of Longtree House, Hurlingham. 'We're in this together and there's no outsider listening. Stop stalling and get down to it.'

The face of the well-dressed man was twisted in mixed dismay and annoyance. A bishop in the flesh could not have done it better.

Carruthers' shoulder was still aching. In him burned a dislike of the well-dressed man and Brown Shoes that might have flared up into a rough-house, but Burke held the cards, in the carriage.

The Bishop's face relaxed a little. He shrugged his shoulders and sighed.

'I've no idea what you're talking about,' he said.

'So you haven't a notion,' Burke remarked.

'I haven't.'

'You didn't deliberately trip my friend?'

'Certainly not, sir!'

'You didn't try to shove him towards the train while pretending to help him?'

'Good heavens, man! It's an outrageous suggestion!'

'And you've never seen that'—Burke jerked a finger towards Brown Shoes—'before?'

'Never.'

Burke shrugged his shoulders, proffered cigarettes to Carruthers and lit up. There was a short silence, broken by Burke's slow words:

'You're a liar,' he said. 'Karen, there are two ways of dealing with you. One is to hand you over to the police, the other is to handle you myself. The police will be considerably more gentle. But if you keep this up . . .'

He stopped. There was a suggestion of fear in the man's eyes, but he stuck to his guns. Brown Shoes was showing more signs of nervousness, but Burke proposed to deal with him later. He could have kept quiet and waited until he had the other men at his flat, where his methods of persuasion could be more convincing. It was probable. But first he was anxious to make the other feel the effect of his methods. Burke knew that his face was set grimly enough to strike fear into stronger men than the Bishop. For it was Burke's intention to let Karen—he was sure it was Karen—get away. Karen would report to someone in higher authority, and that someone needed a healthy respect for the capabilities of Jim Burke.

'My dear sir,' began the Bishop again, 'I don't know whether the unfortunate occurrence on the platform has unhinged you.'

'My dear Karen,' said Burke, icily. 'You tripped my friend deliberately. Now you are going to talk. If you don't . . .' He broke off, and looked at Carruthers. 'Bob—open the door. Wide . . .'

There was a gasp from Brown Shoes as Carruthers obeyed. The face of the benevolent-looking Bishop paled.

'You can't . . .' he began.

'You wouldn't put it to the test,' said Burke. 'There are few things I'd like to read about more than your abrupt end—and your friend's.'

He stopped. The roaring of the train through the tunnel came with trebled force through the open door. Brown Shoes was biting his lips, and the man with the benevolent face was trying to see bluff written on Burke's face.

He didn't see it. With a little gasp like the escape of air from a toy balloon he gave in.

'All right,' he muttered. 'But you'll regret this. You'll suffer for it.'

Burke took as much notice of him as he would an ant.

'You're Adolf Karen,' he said, 'of Longtree House, Hurlingham. Is that right?'

'Yes.'

'I needn't tell you what happened this afternoon,' said Burke, 'but it won't do you any harm to know that I followed you and helped Miss Carris. Incidentally, Miss Carris doesn't know anything. Don't touch her again.'

There was no threat in his words, but Karen licked his lips, as though death was yawning over him. Burke warmed to his job. Karen wasn't a man normally troubled by nerves, but he was cracking.

He went on:

'You're working for Krotz . . .'

Karen gasped again. His eyes were wide open, and it might have been surprise or it might have been fear.

'If you don't clear out of England with your crowd of thugs you'll be wiped out,' Burke said. 'Wiped right out. I'll give you twenty-four hours, not a minute more.'

Karen licked his lips.

'And you can tell Krotz this,' said Burke. 'He's sitting pretty in Lathia, and he thinks he's safe, but he isn't. I know what he's

71

after, and when I've cleared up the other agencies he's running in England, I'm coming after him. Tell him to remember what he did to Carris.'

Burke stopped. Karen was licking his lips again, and his face was a pale pink. The train slowed down at a station and the man looked at the platform, as if imploring help, but no one entered. The train moved on.

'Have you got all that?' asked Burke.

Karen nodded. He looked completely washed out, now, and all the pompousness had gone. Burke took in every detail of his features. Brown Shoes was sitting back in a corner, dread in his eyes, and fear of the open door. The train went on, stopping at station after station, until it reached St. James's Park. Burke stood up.

'I've another little thing to tell you,' he said.

Carruthers saw it coming, and only the warning light in Burke's impassive face stopped him from speaking.

As the four men disgorged themselves from the carriage, Burke in the lead, the big man slipped. His hand, clasping Karen's arm one moment, was pulled away. Carruthers muttered under his breath as Karen flew towards the exit, scattering a dozen passengers. Brown Shoes moved after him.

'Hold him!' snapped Burke.

Carruthers grabbed Brown Shoes. The man almost fell down in his fright, and the passers-by stared at the trio and after the man who had torn past them. But Burke's face told them nothing. Gripping the one captive, he hurried towards the moving stairs. There was no sight of Karen, but Burke didn't expect there would be.

It was just nine o'clock when he reached his Brook Street flat, urging Brown Shoes ahead of him. For a fraction of a second Burke's lips were at Carruthers' ear, and the blond young man smiled and nodded.

'Why don't you get him round to the police?' asked Carruthers, putting the question Burke had prompted. 'It'll save messing about. And we don't want the swine here.'

'I don't want the police in it,' Burke said. 'You don't know half this game, Bob. It's big—and means big money.'

Carruthers grunted. Burke, his great hand round the captive's arm, urged that frightened creature into a chair, and left him to rummage in a drawer of a writing bureau. Carruthers busied himself with a decanter and syphon from the small table in the corner of the room that overlooked Brook Street. This was a typical furnished flat of the W.1 district. The four dining chairs and the gate-leg table were of good quality, the two small tables, sideboard and writing-desk were of well-polished oak. The wooden floor was well polished, too, and the lighting came from an alabaster bowl hanging from the ceiling.

Carruthers brought the drinks.

'Give the poor devil one,' said Burke.

Brown Shoes gulped the drink down with pitiable eagerness. He drew a deep breath when it was finished.

'What's your name?' demanded Burke suddenly.

Brown Shoes didn't hesitate.

'Carter, sir, s'elp me, I never knew . . .'

'Don't talk,' said Burke. 'Unless I ask questions. Where do you live?'

' 'Arndsditch.' The man was thoroughly cowed.

'Street and number?'

'In a flat, sir, top o' Brick Alley. Simpson's Buildings. Yer can't miss 'em.'

'Been there long?'

'Matter o' seven years, on an' orf.'

Burke nodded. A great deal of the grimness that had cowed

Carter disappeared. Burke looked the pleasant and amiable young man about town that he was—sometimes.

'When were you in stir?' he demanded gently.

The man named Carter swallowed hard. But he didn't try to evade the point.

'I came out a coupla' months ago, Mister.'

'What did you go in for?'

'Well, Mister, a man's gotta live. I snitched a coupla' bags from the dames, and got caught.'

'Nothing worse than that?'

'Crorse me throat, sir!'

'Then why,' demanded Burke, suddenly serious, 'do you get mixed up with a crowd of cut-throats like Karen's?'

'I . . .' Carter turned colour. 'I 'ad to, Mister, I 'ad to. An' I never knew there was murder in it—s'elp me!'

'What made you join him?' Burke asked.

He could almost have told Carter his own history. The man had come out of gaol, been paid for a small felony by Karen, and gradually cornered so that if he refused to take Karen's orders he would march back to gaol—if he marched anywhere. He swore that the only hang-out he knew was the Hurlingham one. His only jobs, lately, had been following certain men about London. Burke persuaded him to part with the names and addresses of the men, as far as he knew them.

'You're going to stay here for a little while,' he said. 'And we're going to tie you to a chair, Charlie, because you've got a slippery look about you. Don't try any tricks.'

Just five minutes later Burke was talking to Carruthers in tones loud enough to be overhead. Craigie, or the Arran twins, might have been flummoxed by that conversation.

'It's a pity Karen got away,' Burke said, as he closed the bedroom door. 'But I wasn't ready to deal with him, Bob.

Don't forget we're in between two fires—Karen's and Craigie's.'

Carruthers started to gasp, then began to smile.

'Hmm,' he said.

'Craigie's more dangerous, in England,' went on Burke. 'But I don't think there is likely to be much more trouble over here. Karen will get over to Europe, and he won't want to come back. We'll make sure he's gone, and then get after him.'

'Ah,' said Carruthers, owlishly.

'And we'll have to think up something to do with the little runt in there,' said Burke. 'There's a hell of a lot to do, Bob. Damn. No chicken left—and not much ham. Hungry?'

'I could fork a sausage,' agreed Carruthers.

'We'd better go out for something,' said Burke. 'Charlie'll be all right for an hour—he can meditate on his sins. How's your shoulder?'

'Passing fair,' said Bob Carruthers.

He said, afterwards, that he had the hardest job in his life to keep a straight face and to keep from laughing. Nothing funnier than the seriousness of Burke's share of that conversation had come to him in years. The beauty of it was, opined Carruthers, that it was too simple to fail, always assuming Karen and his crowd knew where Burke lived.

It was more than likely that they had found out, during the afternoon and evening. It was probable the flat was being watched, even then. Burke and Carruthers had considerable respect, by now, for the cleverness of the other side. Thus the trio would have been seen, entering Number 8, Brook Street, and the couple would be seen leaving it. It was reasonable to suppose that some effort would be made to get Carter away from the flat before the return of Burke and Carruthers.

And when Carter saw Karen again, he would talk. Every word of that conversation would get to Karen's ears—every word that mattered, anyhow. And Karen would be half-convinced that Burke and Carruthers were not working for Craigie.

So much Carruthers realised. Even Craigie, when he heard of it a few hours later, wondered whether it wasn't too deep a plot.

The two men, Craigie and Burke, were in Department Z again, and Burke had told his story down to the last detail, not forgetting that everything had worked according to plan, and Carter was gone from the flat. The flat had been entered by a burglar who did a good job; there was hardly a mark on the doors, but the ropes that had bound Carter were in pieces on the bedroom floor.

'I think it'll work,' Burke said.

Craigie rubbed his chin and reached for his inevitable meerschaum.

'Maybe,' he admitted. 'But you're looking three moves ahead.'

'No harm in that, surely.'

Craigie admitted the point.

'And,' he said, 'they had found your address, and they were watching your flat. You backed the right horse until then. Now it remains to be seen whether Krotz bites.'

'Put yourself in his place,' Burke said. 'Wouldn't you? He'll get a report from Karen that there's a third party in the job—Karen, the Department, and myself. He'll pitch a story to Krotz until that swine is getting worked up about the third party. Who is this Burke? He'll be convinced that Burke is dangerous and knows a lot. He'll be told that Burke's threatened to search him out in Lathia. And if the fear of God works in him, he'll do everything he can to make sure Burke doesn't live to visit Lathia. That's reasonable, isn't it?'

Craigie's eyes were shadowed.

'Yes. And if it works, you're safe as a man sitting on a live shell and trying to knock the cap off.'

'That's not the point. It'll keep 'em moving after me. I know you'll say I might have followed Karen and found their second hide-out, but I wouldn't like to back that horse. Don't forget one man was killed this afternoon, because he might have talked. Karen isn't the type to talk much, but if Krotz is on a big enough game, he wouldn't let Karen live, while Karen was being followed. It'd be too dangerous.'

'You're assuming there's someone higher than Karen working in England, are you?'

'I'm assuming there will be, pretty soon,' said Burke. 'Well?'

'Carry on,' said Gordon Craigie. 'And be careful.'

Craigie watched him leave the office, and drew a deep breath. Burke was devastating right enough. Craigie could almost follow his new agent's thoughts. They ran thus:

Krotz was working a game that had interests in England. Krotz was acknowledged to be the most dangerous revolutionary in Europe. Provided he was working on some *coup d'état* that either affected England or needed the help of English capital—the more likely theory—he would stop at nothing to put all obstacles out of his path.

And Krotz would realise he was hopeless against Craigie and his Department, in England. He might be able to deal with Department Z outside England, but he would not make the mistake of trying to beat Craigie's men on their own ground.

He would risk it against Burke, if Burke's ruse had convinced him he was working separately from Department Z.

Craigie didn't know whether the ruse would work. He knew nothing more than Carris had told him about Krotz's recent activities, and that there was a connection between that and the Patricia Carris incident. From that foundation he would normally have progressed slowly, using all the resources of the Department to find some trace of the Lathian activities this side of the North Sea.

But anything which involved Jim Burke wasn't normal.

Craigie smiled as he reached for his pipe. He had known many kinds of courage, and not least was that of Nick Carris, during that last journey to Whitehall. But never had he experienced anything like the courage of Jim Burke, who had, after all, sent an invitation for a call from death.

8

VARIOUS SIDES TO A QUESTION

Figuratively, Jim Burke had stuck his head over the parapet and invited trouble, but it didn't worry him. He was more concerned at the possibility that Karen would have decided already he was a Department Z agent. There were good reasons for such an assumption. Karen wouldn't be easily convinced that the Longtree House raid was the work of an independent man; knowing Carris had been an agent, he would naturally assume Burke knew him through the Department. The funny part of the whole business, Burke told Carruthers, was that he, Burke, had obviously been a Z man during the Hurlingham do—but he *hadn't* been—and yet Karen might reasonably doubt whether he was a Z man on the Walham Green showing—when he *had* been.

There was, of course, always the chance that Carruthers, Burke and the Arrans had been seen going from the Arrans' flat to Whitehall, but that affair had been so early in the day that Burke doubted whether Karen's crowd had picked up his trail by then. The second visit to Whitehall, and Department

Z, would have given the other side a better opportunity—but Burke was confident that he had evaded any possible shadow before he had made that visit.

All these things he told an unusually serious Carruthers, towards ten o'clock that night, while he was sitting in a corner of the Mayday Club.

The Mayday Club is a restaurant-cum-night club, moderately well run and free from the likelihood of a police raid. Its dancing-cum-dining-room was large and square, with wall lighting effects of pleasant and changing colours, perfect waiters, exquisite food and wines and a clientele that could only be called distinguished. It was a popular club, and Burke was continually nodding to acquaintances who turned in a cramped space under a vague impression that they were dancing.

Burke was looking at a girl whose back and shoulders gleamed white and attractive. She was dressed in black, her hair was very dark and two pink lobes peeped fascinatingly beneath a cluster of ringlets on either side of her head. She was dancing with a tall, middle-aged man, distinguished of bearing, who was devoting all his attentions to his partner. Burke regarded them idly.

'Even assuming,' said Carruthers, a little plaintively, 'Karen and his crowd bite, Jim, how much better off are you?'

'I don't know—yet.'

Carruthers' fair hair glistened beneath the lights, and his pleasant face had a look of unmistakable dissatisfaction. He believed Burke was keeping something back and he felt he deserved his friend's full confidence.

'And even,' he said, 'if you are any better off, why come to this hole-in-corner for fun? It's as dead as a dodo.'

Burke beckoned a waiter.

'Bob,' he said, 'you're a good soul, but an innocent one. Supposing Karen's watching us? What's he likely to do?'

'Wait outside until we leave.'

'Why shouldn't he come inside and watch us?'

'Who? Karen? He won't dare to show his face for a long time.'

'It won't be Karen in person, it'll be one of his tribe,' Burke reasoned.

Carruthers scowled.

'Can you imagine Carter or his kidney crashing in here? Have some sense.'

'I don't expect Carter, but I think we're being watched, even now. Somewhere in this hive of pleasure men or women are watching us. Some glowing-eyed goddess will lure us on.'

'Bats,' said Carruthers, bluntly.

'We'll get something for our money, before we leave here,' Burke prophesied. 'You need a more trusting mind, Bob.'

He stopped.

Carruthers, wrinkling his nose in disgust, saw the hardening of his friend's eyes.

'Don't look at me like that, idiot,' Burke growled.

Carruthers scowled.

'That's better,' said Burke. 'The tall, good-looking cove, Bob, and the girl in black. The girl's side-face to us now.'

Carruthers drained his glass while looking at the crowd of dancers. He saw the man and the girl, and had a shock.

'Good gosh!' he muttered.

Burke nodded. That was how he felt—incredible though it seemed. Patricia Carris was dancing at the Mayday Club, on the night of her brother's death.

She was smiling, too, as if happy.

Her companion, the middle-aged and distinguished-looking man, was obviously in the seventh heaven.

Jim Burke drained his glass. He felt hot and sticky at the neck, and his fingers drummed on the table. Carruthers pushed a hand through his fair hair, and gave it up.

When Bart Hemming suggested an evening at the May-day Club, Patricia Carris meant to say 'no'. A word to Hemming about the death of Nick would have been more than sufficient excuse. She had known Hemming only a few weeks, it was true, but she had learned to expect from him courtesy and consideration in all things.

He was tall, more than usually handsome, old enough to carry himself with distinction, and, apparently, as rich as Croesus.

That night, everything that had happened seemed very far away.

Hemming had called at the Lord's Avenue house a month before. She hadn't known him, but she had welcomed him when he said he had news from her brother. True, the news hadn't been startling. At that time Nick had been in Central Europe and Bart Hemming had met him, casually, and had promised to bring the message to his sister. Patricia couldn't imagine why Nick hadn't written, but she had received messages from him in a dozen different ways, and she wasn't surprised by the messenger.

Hemming had suggested they should dine together.

How many times had she dined or lunched with him since? She didn't remember. She had been too concerned about Nick's long absence to think a great deal about anything else. She did know that the genial, happy-go-lucky young men of her acquaintance would have driven her crazy, and she had turned to Hemming with real relief.

Perhaps Hemming realised it; at any rate, he appeared to derive ample enjoyment from her company.

And then he had come that night, the night of Nick's death. Friendly and somehow dependable, it occurred to her that she might find some respite from the mental torment of the knowledge that Nick was dead. And something else had occurred to her.

She found it hard to define, even as they dined and danced. She kept smiling and laughing, with a kind of desperation, and all the time she was wondering how she should talk to Bart. Should she confide in him?

Suddenly she compared him with the big, serious-faced Burke. If she confided in Burke she could imagine that he would tell her to dismiss the idea from her mind, and, if she still clung to it, contrive a means to get her away from London where she could do nothing mad. But Hemming, who knew nothing of the circumstances, might help.

She wanted to avenge Nick.

It was absurd, of course. It was madness. But she ached to find the men who had caused his murder. Further than that she dared not think.

They were dancing to a slow waltz, but the music hardly reached her ears and her limbs moved stiffly. There was a confused babble about her, only because of Hemming's guidance did she avoid banging into a dozen couples. Until she saw Burke.

He was sitting with a fair-headed man at a corner table, and he was staring at her. Something in his expression seemed to freeze her. She leaned heavily against Hemming.

He smiled down at her.

'What is it, Pat?' He had a pleasant, low-pitched voice.

'I'd like to go home,' she said, hurriedly. 'Quickly, please. I'll tell you why, later.'

Hemming led her towards their table, paid the bill, took her to the foyer and, as she came from the cloak-room, held her arm as they hurried into the street to the waiting taxi. He knew exactly when to talk and when to keep silent.

'We'll soon be there,' he said, as the taxi moved.

She flashed a quick smile and nodded.

Hemming did not look behind him, and if he had he would not have been able to tell if the cab was being followed. Nor would he have recognised Carruthers, sitting at the back of a second cab. Carruthers was lighting a cigarette and wondering whether Burke *did* know what he was doing. Burke's words, as Patricia Carris and her companion had threaded their way between the tables, had been brief.

'Get after 'em, Bob. See 'em both home before you go back to my flat.'

The two cabs went through the frosty brilliance of London's West End, while the March wind cut the people in the streets to their marrows.

There was little of 'the bishop' about Adolf Karen as he sat in the front room of a small, detached house in Wembley and looked at the stubby figure of the man Carter. Karen's eyes were hard and glittering, and his lips were thin. There was no benevolence in his face. Smoke curled from a cigar between his thumb and forefinger. Carter was five feet away from him, fidgeting on a small chair opposite.

'And Burke didn't pay you for these lies?' Karen's voice was hard.

'S'elp me, Mister, it's Gawd's truth! Every word, as I sit 'ere. I wouldn't lie, Mister. That's wot 'e said . . .'

Karen looked towards a massive man standing by the door.

'Did Carter have any money on him, Hermann?'

The massive man shook his head.

'A few shillings, Mr. Karen.'

'I see,' murmured Karen, looking back at Carter. 'If you've lied, you've written your name on a bullet. If you want to correct anything, say so now.'

Carter's eyes were screwed up.

'Honest to Gawd, Mister . . .'

'Send him to the others,' ordered Karen.

Gustav Hermann opened the door, waited for Carter and followed him up the stairs to a large room, intended for a bedroom but turned into a smoking-room-cum-café by the several men who lounged in easy chairs and read paper-backed American magazines or a periodical from Paris. No one looked round as Carter entered, or when the door closed, and Hermann went back to Karen.

Carter made for a whisky bottle standing on a table. A swallow of neat spirit steadied him. The colour came back to his cheeks, and he grunted:

'Friendly lot, aincha?'

One of the others turned. His right hand was bandaged, where Burke's bullet had wounded him earlier in the day. Burke would have recognised three of them, as well as Gustav Hermann, as occupants of Longtree House.

'Siddown, Bud,' he said cheerfully, 'and don't go too heavy on the waggon. Been having a bright time?'

'Bright time, huh,' grunted Carter. 'I dunno' whether you know Burke, but he's sent some shivers down me spine, and that ain't a lie.'

'Burke?' The three men who had been lined up against the wall of Longtree House looked at Carter with fresh interest. 'James William Burke, now and for ever at your service.' The mocking voice of the big man who had held them up seemed to echo through the room.

'Spill it,' said the man with the bandaged hand.

Carter, encouraged by a receptive audience and another spot of whisky, recounted his day's adventures. There was an air of tension in the room, and no one interrupted the story. At last:

'That man's poison,' finished Carter, 'you can take it from me.'

'Sure,' said the American, thoughtfully. 'We can take it from him, too. I reckon we're going to be busy, boys.'

He grinned. For the first time, that glassy expression revealed itself in his eye and was reflected in the eyes of the others, excepting Carter. A huge, blond man whistled between broken teeth and took an automatic from his pocket, polishing it with a handkerchief. Carter shivered, but said nothing.

It would be a long time, Gustav Hermann admitted to himself, before he forgot the fear that the man Burke had put into him.

Karen looked up as his servant entered the room.

'Think Carter's lying?' he demanded.

Hermann shrugged his big shoulders. His oily face was expressionless.

'Can't tell, Boss. But Burke's a big boy.'

'I don't need telling that,' Karen growled. 'He made you look the biggest fool in Europe. I haven't forgotten it.'

Hermann's face paled.

'That's right,' he admitted. 'But he caught the others, don't forget, and if he can line three of them up like that, I didn't do so badly.'

Karen shrugged.

'According to Carter,' he said, half to himself, 'Burke's not working with Craigie.'

'I tried him out, too. He didn't bat an eye when I mentioned Craigie.'

'You're sure of that?' Karen demanded.

'As sure as I'm here.'

'But he told me to remember Carris,' Karen objected. Again he seemed to be speaking to himself, and again Hermann broke in eagerly:

'Yes, but he followed you from the girl's place, Boss— Carris's place. Maybe he was watching the girl because of her brother.'

Karen nodded. It was possible.

'And Carter picked him up outside Lord's Avenue,' went on Hermann, anxiously. 'So he was still watching there.'

Karen remembered the affair at the station, when he had followed Carter and the man Carruthers, when Carruthers had been snatched back from the live rails, and when Burke had forced him to suffer that journey.

Apart from that one reference to Carris, and the general circumstances by which Karen assumed anyone who worked against him was an agent of Gordon Craigie's, there was nothing to link Burke and his fair-headed friend to the Department. Generally, it looked as if Burke was working on his own.

And Burke knew about Krotz.

Karen felt afraid when he thought of that. He was the chief agent of the Lathian minister in England, but he knew he would receive no mercy if Krotz once imagined he was failing on his job. There was so much to be done that he wished it hadn't been necessary to use force.

But it *had* been necessary. If the police had questioned the victim of the machine-gun shooting, the man would have talked. Karen would have found himself hemmed in, with the Hurlingham and Wembley hideouts known to the police. It would have meant failure.

After all, he reasoned, Krotz himself had insisted on the

gunmen being organised. Everything Karen had done in England had been done under cover of the gunmen. But until Carris had escaped, and started for England, there had been no hitch. If Carris had been kept in Lathia, Karen knew, he would have had no trouble in England. It was Krotz's fault that the trouble had developed.

It wasn't going to help, to blame Krotz. The only way Karen could ensure his own safety was to win against Burke and Craigie's men. Otherwise it would mean death, Karen knew. Others, before him, had failed Krotz, and had died. Krotz never revealed his whole strength, even to his own side. In England, despite Karen and his organisation, there were two or three other agents, watching everything, checking Karen's work. Krotz would probably know already of the shooting affair, and the discovery of Longtree House.

'Is Burke being watched?' Karen demanded suddenly.

'Yes.' Hermann was suave. 'I put Rogers and Lister on him. I reasoned they could go where he can go, without any trouble.'

Karen nodded. Rogers and Lister were men of the same class as Burke and Carruthers, and could gain admittance to any place in London. Hermann was sharp—a very useful man. But he couldn't afford to spare Rogers and Lister to watch Burke for long. They were needed for other work. Of course it would be easy enough to get rid of Burke and Carruthers, but would it be wise? Or were they being shadowed by Craigie's men, were they actually English agents? Was it safer to let them go for a while?

Karen's eyes were like steel as he looked up at Hermann and snapped 'Get out.' Hermann nodded and hurried away. Karen took a wallet from his pocket, extracted a thin piece of folded paper, and, taking a pencil from his desk, began to write.

It took him half an hour to finish. The code from which he was working was a difficult one, and the message he was sending to Krotz was complicated. He took the telephone from his desk, and called the Western Union Cables Company. Ten minutes later an apparently innocent message from the London firm of Smethwick and Karen was being transmitted to the Lathian smelting works of that company. Actually, it was to Krotz, summarising the position and asking advice on the next step.

Karen believed in playing for safety.

A blizzard howled and whined across the Baltic Sea, venting its full force on Rikka and the coast of Lathia, covering the town in a thick carpet of snow, piercing everyone who ventured out with a wind that cut like a knife. Very few people walked the wide, icy streets. Even the military police were huddled in corners and doorways, out of the blast. Beyond the limits of the town, the countryside was a barren white waste. Occasionally a blast of wind would sweep the snow from the leafless trees, streaking a skeleton of black against the blanket, but in a few minutes the snow had turned black to white again. No car ventured along the roads leading from Rikka, but here and there a white mound revealed a stranded vehicle, and a gloved hand stretched out of a partly opened window to clear the snow away and freshen the air inside. Two miles from the town, a smaller mound covered a woman who had been caught by the storm, had floundered, staggered, fallen and finally frozen to death.

It seemed that nothing could live in that desolation.

Towards morning the wind dropped and the snow fell in smaller flakes. The freezing air cleared. At four o'clock a little procession of men turned from the fields at the side of the road that led to Rikka and past the villa of Marius Krotz.

There were three men, wrapped in furs, fighting against the soft, crisp snow beneath their snowshoes, making progress slowly, but making it all the same.

Krotz's villa reared up against the grey sky, a squat building covered with snow, which was heaped against the sides of the house and the windows. No lights twinkled, but the three men reached the front door, clearing the waist-high snow and banging on the heavy knocker. There was a shuffle of sound beyond. A liveried footman opened the door, peered at the faces of the callers and stood back for them to pass.

The leader, a man as big as Burke, stumped into the hall, and the white covering of his furs melted against the onslaught of sudden warmth. He took off his coat and leggings, stiffly, helped by the footman. His companions managed by themselves. He stood revealed, five minutes after his arrival, as a huge, gorilla of a man, with a straggly black beard and a pair of penetrating, cruel eyes.

'Tell him I'm here,' he growled. His voice was gruff and arrogant.

The footman bowed and turned away. The big man and his companions warmed their cold limbs against the blazing log fire in the hall, grunting when a second footman hurried towards them with vodka. The drink warmed their vitals. They talked gruffly, cursing the blizzard and the man who had made them come out in it.

They stopped grumbling as the first footman reappeared.

'You will follow me, Herra Marx?'

The big man followed the footman. They went up the wide stairs, along a passage of pseudo-marble and stopped at a red-painted door. The footman tapped. A thin voice said:

'Send Marx in, Piet.'

Marx pushed open the door and entered the bedroom of Marius Krotz.

Krotz realised that to look ridiculous was the most damaging thing in the eyes of his supporters, and he had dressed quickly in a black coat and a pair of morning trousers that might have been fresh from Savile Row. He wore a white silk cravat pinned with a single pearl.

A man of fifty-two, Marius Krotz carried his years well. Whatever revolutionary and political excess he had committed, he was an ascetic towards the sins of the flesh. He was nearly six feet tall, a thick-set man with very square shoulders, and only the suggestion of a stomach beneath his black waistcoat. But few men could see him and think of his clothes or his figure. His eyes held the attention.

They were black, with a yellow tinge at the edges. Set wide apart beneath brows that sloped upwards to the temples, they gave him the appearance of a man perpetually inquisitive. And they burned with an inward light, even while the rest of his face was impassive. His nose was small and slightly on one side, and his forehead looked like a shallow V, dipping between his raised, black brows. Incongruously, he was completely bald, a feature his eyebrows emphasised. His lips were thin and compressed, with the corners higher than the middle, again in a shallow V. His chin was square and hard-jowled, with the point making the V that characterised his features.

His skin was pale and very clear.

Marx closed the door behind him. Krotz, sitting at a small table, pushed a box of thin cigarettes towards the messenger. Those who met Marius Krotz and knew his reputation were astonished by his leisurely manner; he looked like a man whom nothing could hurry.

'Smoke, Marx.' His voice was still high and thin. 'A bad night for travelling.'

Marx grunted. He was an ill-favoured man, quite fearless—and loyal to Krotz.

'Yes, filthy,' he rasped. 'But there was a message from England at the factory, Herra Krotz. It had to be brought.'

He took the cablegram from his big pocket, and waited while Krotz read it. The power behind the Lathian throne murmured to himself, stood up and went to the wall safe. He ignored Marx, as Marx ignored him, as he took a thin piece of paper, fellow to that Karen had used a few hours before, and used his pencil on the cypher. Then he read the message, without any expression.

It ran:

Longtree House raided by two men, James Burke, Robert Carruthers. Both unknown, not believed agents British Service. Necessary to use force. B and C not touched. Do you advise further force? K.

The pink tongue of Marius Krotz crept along his lips for a moment. He opened another sheet of paper, taken from the safe, a cable received from England earlier, before the blizzard had howled from the sea. It was similar to the second cable, with the important addition of:

. . . Believe Burke and Carruthers dangerous. Assume Burke was waiting for Carris at Carris home. Carris reached Whitehall, no further. Advise allow Karen handle B and C immediately. Instruct. 3.

Krotz tapped the top of his desk with white, heavy fingers, then pressed a communication bell. There was a pause, while Marx and his leader stared towards the log fire in the magnificent hearth. Everything about the villa outside Rikka was magnificent, in size and quality.

A door opened at last. A short, thin-faced man entered the room, with a furtive, almost frightened air. He was well-favoured, facially, and few would have hesitated to classify him as English. Krotz spoke as soon as the newcomer had closed the door.

'Matthews. You know the English Service well?'

The man named Matthews shrugged.

'Well enough, Herra Krotz.'

'Do the names Burke and Carruthers convey anything to you? Burke—and Carruthers?'

Matthews rubbed his chin. His light blue eyes flickered.

'No—not in the Service, Herra Krotz. But Burke—it might be James Burke—a big man.'

'James. Yes. That's him.'

'The big man,' Matthews said, his eyes still flickering. 'He was in Madrid when I was there, Herra Krotz. He is big enough to blunder into anything.'

'He is not an official agent?'

Matthews shrugged.

'I would be prepared to say he was not, but it isn't certain. Yet I doubt it. Burke has always been by himself when Craigie has been busy, and Craigie would have used him if possible.'

Krotz nodded. The yellowish edge to his black eyes grew wider, and he smiled.

'All right, Matthews,' he said.

Before the Englishman had left the room, Krotz was working on a message. Ten minutes passed before he handed it to Marx, coded and ready for transmission. He said:

'Eat before you leave here and then send this message, from the factory. It must go within two hours.'

Marx grunted and stood up. As the door closed behind his

vast frame, Krotz snapped his fingers, sharply. Marx pushed open the door again.

'You called me, Herra Krotz?'

Krotz smiled.

'What is your opinion of our agent, Karen, Marx?'

The big man scowled, rubbed his hairy hands together and grunted:

'Karen is dirt, Herra Krotz. He works for himself always. But he is clever. That is all.'

Krotz nodded, and the door closed again.

It was noon on the following day that Karen, in the London office of the steel manufacturing company of Smethwick and Karen, received the message from Lathia. He did not look like Adolf Karen, for he affected a brown beard, to match his hair, and a pair of thin, rimless glasses. In the office he was known as an accountant from the Newcastle works of the company, for Karen had long since realised the necessity for a cover behind which he could, if necessary, get lost.

He de-coded the message, hurriedly burned the cable, left the office and went to a house in Wembley.

It was a house of medium size, standing in its own grounds and, according to the notice-board outside, it offered board-residence to gentlemen. A man whom Burke knew as Gustav Hermann opened the front door. Karen waited until the door was closed, and then snapped:

'Tell the others to get ready, Hermann.'

Hermann, with his hand bandaged still, nodded and hurried upstairs.

Just half an hour later three men went from the house,

going singly but meeting at a small garage, half a mile away, and getting into a closed Daimler car. They had instructions to kill . . .

For the message Karen had read:

Destroy Burke and Carruthers. Report through Number 3.

9

BURKE GETS CROSS

No one less like a man under sentence of death could be imagined than James William Burke as he let himself out of his Brook Street flat at nine-thirty on the morning after the visit to the Mayday Club. For a big man he had always been scrupulous about his clothes, and he wore dark grey worsted, grey-striped shirt and socks and a grey-spotted tie. His crisp, dark hair was bared to the wan sun of March, his eyes were agleam, and his generous lips were parted as he hummed a three-year-old ditty.

He had received three telephone calls that morning, and had argued with himself for most of the night. The calls in a small degree and his arguments in a large one brought him to the conclusion that whatever the motive of Pat Carris's Mayday Club visit, it had not been concerned with the Krotz affair. In fact, with the sun shining on him he could hardly imagine how he had ever believed it possible. He *had* been shocked to find her there, but human reactions to grief were many and strange.

The telephone calls filled his mind as he walked towards Oxford Street.

First, at one-fifteen he had been called by a weary and irritable Carruthers. Carruthers had followed the girl and her escort to 17, Lord's Avenue, and he said, with a touch of malice, that contrary to expectations the parting on the doorstep had been brief and formal. Thereafter he had followed the middle-aged man to the Krazy Kat club, a recent, daring and expensive establishment in Bond Street. He, Carruthers, had waited outside until his quarry had reappeared, and at twelve forty-five he had seen his man disappear into the American Club.

'American,' Burke had muttered.

'I chatted with the night clerk there,' Carruthers had said. 'Our man's name is Bartholomew Hemming, and he's rich. He's been living at the Club, on and off, for six months.'

'Is that the lot?'

There had been a pause.

'The lot!' Carruthers had bellowed. 'The lot!'

'You're highly commended,' Burke had chuckled. 'Good night, and be ready by nine in the morning.'

At two o'clock he had been called by Gordon Craigie, and he had asked a question that every agent who had worked for Craigie had asked, sooner or later.

'Don't you ever sleep?' he had demanded.

'Not when I'm busy,' Craigie had said. 'Listen.'

The first few sentences made Burke aware, for the first time, of the thoroughness of Department Z. Apparently he and Carruthers had been shadowed throughout the day, and their visit to the Mayday Club had been reported. What was more interesting, both of them had been followed from the club, by others as well as Craigie's men!

'Carruthers was followed by a man named Rogers,' said

Craigie. 'He's supposed to be a private detective, divorce cases mostly, but I've often wondered whether he's mixed up in anything else. Rogers followed Carruthers to the Krazy Kat and American Club, then home. My man followed Rogers to his flat in Albemarle Street.'

'He makes a lot of money, for a private detective, if he can live there,' Burke had remarked.

'Yes. Well, a Jacob Lister followed you. Lister's an ex-officer, used for Intelligence during the War, but we haven't made use of him since. He drinks too much. He followed you to Brook Street, waited for half an hour outside, then went to his home in Chelsea. He's married, by the way.'

'Did you know anything about the Walham Green incident from your men, apart from what I told you?' asked Burke.

'No. You were lost across London. But listen, Burke. I'm sending you photographs of Rogers and Lister, and you can make sure whether they're following you, after today. I won't tail you, unless you'd rather.'

'I don't mind,' Burke said. 'Better let Carruthers have a cover, though. Bob gets hot-tempered, at times.'

Craigie had laughed and rung off.

The third call had come from Scotland Yard, and Burke was told that his flat had been visited during the evening by two men, who, it was believed, had broken in. The detective who had been watching the Brook Street flat had made no effort to stop them, as he was told by Superintendent Miller to hold a watching brief only. The detective had, Burke learned, been run down by a car, soon after leaving Brook Street, and his report had only just been received. No, he wasn't badly hurt.

After this orgy of telephoning, Burke had gone to sleep. At nine-thirty this morning, he left his flat and strode towards Oxford Street. The gleam in his eyes might have been accounted for by the fact that he was going to visit Patricia Carris. He was fairly confident that there would be no immediate trouble from Karen, and he wanted to visit Patricia before the real work started. He could not rid himself of the idea that her trip to the Mayday Club had been for some purpose apart from pleasure, and he wanted to confirm it.

Patricia was finishing a late breakfast. She was dressed in a heather mixture cardigan suit that fitted her to perfection, and she was pale and weary-eyed.

Her smile, as they shook hands, was a little uncertain.

'You'll have some coffee?' she asked.

'May I?'

She poured coffee, and while he was stirring his, she said:

'I suppose you saw me last night?'

Burke gave his nicest grin.

'Yes.'

It was difficult to understand her expression.

'I suppose you're wondering how I could go there, with Nick's funeral tomorrow. Please—please don't laugh when I tell you why I went out.'

'You needn't,' Burke protested quickly.

'But I want to. You see, I've known Bart Hemming for some weeks, and he knew Nick slightly. I felt I could talk to him about Nick's murder.' Her voice was suddenly hard. 'I want to *do* something. It's horrible, sitting here, hating the fact that he's dead. I feel I'd like to kill whoever did it. Kill them! You can understand, can't you?'

Burke was very sober as he looked at her.

'More than that,' he said. 'I half expected it. Tell me, did you talk to Hemming?'

She shook her head.

'No. I couldn't, after all.'

That was one piece of good news.

'Pat,' Burke said, using her Christian name for the first time, but with the easy confidence of an old friend, 'if you let yourself do things like that, you're asking for trouble. Nick's death was a blow. But stand up to it. Don't complicate things by trying to help. You're not used to the game, and if the other side thought you were in the way they'd have as much mercy on you as they would a fly. And it might be that I couldn't help. I don't doubt Hemming is a useful man in a lot of ways, but if he came into a thing like this, unknowing, he'd be committing suicide.'

All the time Patricia's eyes had been on his, and she had listened to the quiet, convincing voice. He had the manner of a man to whom nothing was impossible.

There was a pause.

'Yes,' she said, in a very low voice.

Burke smiled reassuringly.

'That's fine,' he said. 'Now, you don't mind me butting in?'

'Of course not!'

'Who's looking after things, for Nick?' he asked. 'Of course, the manner of his death is hushed up. But you've friends or relatives?'

'An aunt and uncle are coming from Scotland,' she said. 'They'll be here this afternoon. I shall be all right.'

Burke nodded.

'And afterwards?'

'I haven't decided.'

'If I were you,' said Burke gently, 'I'd go back with them for a week or two. It will do you good.'

She flashed an unexpected smile.

'Make me safe?'

'There's a lot to be said for that, too. Will you?'

She hesitated for a moment, then nodded.

'All right,' she said. 'They'll want me to, I know.'

Burke smiled and stood up. He felt more relieved than he would have admitted, even to himself. He was about to say 'goodbye' when the idea came into his mind, pushing everything else out.

'Now—why not come for a drive? It'll blow the cobwebs away. I can have a car round in ten minutes.'

She looked at him for a moment and then smiled.

'I'll be ready,' she said. 'The phone's in that corner.'

There was colour in Patricia's cheeks and a sparkle in her eyes as the Bentley Burke had hired raced along the deserted country roads, past stretches of farmland, green meadows smiling in the sun, bare branches of trees with their promise of coming spring. They stopped at a roadside café in Sussex about noon, and Burke talked.

They had an immense meal and at one o'clock they started back.

There was a difference, now. He sensed Patricia was fighting against reality. The shadow of the tragedy was over her, and she could not escape it. The miles passed behind them as Burke cursed the need for returning to London.

Just outside Kingston he saw the Daimler saloon.

His mind clicked back. He had no time to think, hardly time to act, for the thing came on him with devastating suddenness. If he hadn't recognised the driver he might not have lived to realise anything, but he remembered the expressionless face of the man who had driven a Daimler saloon past him on the previous day. Fear scorched through his mind, less for himself than for the girl. And savage anger was with it.

It was useless to duck. The Daimler could pass them and

fire downwards into the low-lying Bentley. There was only one thing for it.

He wrenched at the wheel. Patricia gasped and clung to the door. Burke rammed into the hedge, bellowing:

'Cover your face!'

The hedge loomed in front of her. She ducked, burying her head in her arms, and then the Bentley tore through the bracken and bramble, shivering and snorting. Thorns caught her sleeves, her back, her hair, but she hardly noticed them.

From behind there came a deadly *tap-tap-tap-tap*.

The Bentley stopped. Burke's hand was in his pocket and out again in a flash, holding a gun. He screwed round, seeing the Daimler passing them, and the hard eyes of the man he had wounded, on the previous day, staring from the rear. A Thomson sub-machine gun was spurting fire, but the bullets were pecking into the grass verge. The target had changed too quickly for the gun to be levelled.

Burke's gun spoke. Glass cracked, by the gunman's head, but doing no other damage. The Daimler raced on, scattering traffic right and left, and before Burke could fire again, it was out of range.

People were shouting, cars were pulling up, a frightened man with a red face peered over the hedge.

'Are you all right?'

Burke looked at Patricia, and saw the last thing he expected. A smile.

He grinned at the red-faced man.

'We're fine!' he said.

10

GENTLEMEN OF THE BOARD

The thing was so big that Burke nearly missed it, and for once Craigie was late in seeing it. They discussed it three days after the shooting affair on the Kingston road, following forty-eight hours of comparative peace.

Burke had taken Patricia safely back to London and, on the following evening, had watched her entering the Flying Scot, with a genial Scotsman and a chubby little woman, her uncle and aunt. He could conceive of no reason why Karen should want to harm her. He did not admit it, but he had felt a slight resentment at the presence of Bart Hemming on the platform, but he could not reasonably complain, even to himself. And, he admitted, Hemming looked a nice chap.

It was Superintendent Horace Miller who checked the American's history, and presented a satisfactory report to Burke and Craigie as they sat in Department Z. The report read:

Name: Bartholomew Hemming.

Age: 49.

Nationality: American.

Born: New Jersey.

Occupation: Controlling director Hemming Rolling Mills, New Jersey.

Income: Uncertain. Reputed dollar millionaire.

Notes: Has been travelling Europe for three months on long vacation, following serious illness. A frequent visitor to England during past ten years. Business visits. Vouched for by New York Police, identity confirmed by members American Club, Piccadilly.

'Of course,' said Craigie, 'there was no reason to suspect Hemming.'

'His meeting with Carris in Europe seems odd,' said Burke, offering cigarettes to Miller.

'We have to send messages by all routes,' Craigie said, 'and a personal message like that was as safe as any. Carris realised his letters might have been opened. That's why he didn't report here at all. No, there's nothing to arouse suspicion, but if you like you can tackle Hemming about his meeting with Carris.'

Burke nodded.

'By the way,' said Miller as he turned to leave the office, 'is Carruthers all right?'

'He's getting restive,' Burke said, 'but he wants to shake your hand. He'd have been in Queer Street but for your men.'

'He's not the only one,' said Miller cheerfully.

The attack on Carruthers had come as quickly as that on Burke. The fair-haired man had entered his flat in Audley Street about half past one on the day of the Kingston affair, and reappeared in the street ten minutes afterwards. Simultaneously, a Daimler saloon had moved from the kerb. The Scotland Yard man who had been watching Carruthers had bellowed a warning. Carruthers had ducked, getting a scalp wound; his saviour had invited trouble by a plucky attempt to intercept the car, and had been lucky to get no more than the two bullet holes drilled through his shoulder.

Burke had hurried to Carruthers' flat on returning to London and had discovered the extent of the injury. He had told himself that it served to prove one thing. Karen had two Daimlers, and two sets of gunmen.

Burke had been sorely tempted, in the three days that followed, to regret his decision to let Karen get away. But he had found support from Craigie.

'The two escapes will make him nervous,' Craigie had said. 'Don't let it worry you, Burke. Karen wouldn't have led you to a place that's important, he's too shrewd. By the way, I want to talk to you. Will you come tomorrow?'

Burke had made sure that he wasn't followed to Whitehall, and entered Department Z by means of a rarely used private door that led through miles, it seemed, of stone passages before it reached Craigie's office. Miller had been waiting, and the Hemming possibility had been reviewed.

Craigie drew up a second armchair as Miller left the office, and the two men sat each side of a cheerful fire while Craigie asked:

'Have you found anything at all to suggest what it's all about?'

'No,' said Burke.

'Any theories?'

'I haven't much time for 'em,' Burke said frankly, 'but I get an idea now and again, and I had one half an hour ago. We've been setting our caps at Karen all the time, forgetting he's a partner in a prominent firm of steel workers. Did it strike you like that?'

Craigie nodded, a little ruefully.

'It wasn't until this morning that I thought it best to check up on Smethwick, Karen's partner,' he said. 'I can give you brief particulars.'

In a report similar to the Yard's report on Hemming, Burke read that Nathaniel Smethwick was a Yorkshireman of sixty-five years of age, that he had travelled very little outside the country, and that he had been bred, and very nearly born, in the Newcastle works of his firm. His father had run the business, building it from next to nothing, and Smethwick himself had only taken Karen into the business because the ex-Pole was able to negotiate for certain Lathian iron-ore rights. The Lathian ore being very nearly the best obtainable, Smethwick and Karen ran a very profitable business.

'But Karen and Smethwick hold only fifty-one per cent of the shares between 'em,' said Burke, as he finished the report. 'Any idea who the other directors are?'

Craigie handed a slip of paper to his new agent. Burke squinted at it. A certain Colonel Bilton and the Hon. Marcus Cassey made up the board of directors.

'Know them?' asked Burke.

'Guinea pigs on a dozen companies,' said Craigie.

Burke screwed up his nose.

'I'll give them the once-over,' he promised, with that unconscious air of being capable of putting the whole thing right when he had time.

'Are you going to see Hemming?'

'I want to know when and where he saw Nick Carris,' said Burke. 'Anything else?'

'How's the Lathian language?' Craigie asked.

Burke pulled a face.

'A headache,' he said, and Craigie chuckled as his agent left by that secret and circuitous route to Whitehall.

It was half past two, and March was blowing with a filibustering inconsistency. Burke enjoyed battling against it, but blue noses and clutched hats were the rule in the streets. He made his way to the Carilon Club, and sought a *Who's Who* in the reading room. As he expected, both Colonel Arthur Martin Bilton, O.M., C.B.E. and the Hon. Reginald Palfrey Marcus Cassey, only son of Lord Marcus Cassey, were men of middle age and members of the Carilon Club. He confirmed that they were on the boards of a dozen different industrial companies, and an hour's talk with the Colonel, who was in the smoking room, convinced him that the man would never be capable of conspiracy, strong or mild. Bilton was a peppery little man, who had seen service in India, and who was prepared to talk for ever. Burke steered the conversation round to the steel company, and mentioned Karen.

'Ah!' said Bilton, 'demmed nice feller, demmed nice. Ah! You know him, Burke?'

'I met him abroad,' said Burke affably. 'Is he in London now?'

'As far as I know. Can't be sure,' said the Colonel, and then, inspired: 'Ring the office, and find out. Demmit, he ought to be, come to think of it. Smethwick's ill.'

'Sorry to hear that,' murmured Burke. 'Nothing serious, is it?'

'Demmed touchy old codger, between ourselves, Burke. I don't think he's quite—er—quite . . .'

Burke rubbed his chin and stored this interesting piece of

news for future reference. Bilton apparently wondered whether he had been wise to confide in a man who was no more than a club acquaintance, and hurried on. For a man who usually talked for hours and said nothing, he was doing well.

'And Cassey's up in Scotland—trouble with his people—old man's ill, maybe you've seen it.' Bilton delivered himself of these things in disconnected and somewhat breathless phrases. 'So Karen's running the London office—assistant managing director, you know.'

'Smethwick's not in London?' asked Burke, feeling safe enough to put any question to the red-faced and breathless Colonel.

'Oh, yes. At Hampstead.'

'There's one thing,' said Burke sympathetically, 'you can always rely on the executive staff to look after these things, can't you?'

It would have taken the prize for ambiguity with anyone but the Colonel, who shrugged and scowled.

'Don't trust anyone, Burke. Cut-throat business, these days. Of course, we haven't much staff in London. Clerk, couple of girl typists. And Cuthbertson comes down pretty often, but Karen is *chargé d'affaires*, you follow me?'

'Oh, quite.' Burke offered cigarettes. 'Fine old Yorkshire name, Cuthbertson.'

'Is it?' asked the Colonel, without interest. 'He's another one like Smethwick. Usually manages to barge down when Karen's not there and calls for me, for some demmed fool reason. Speaks through his beard and you can't understand him.'

It was obvious that Colonel Bilton found the London office of the Smethwick and Karen Company something of a nuisance and Burke left the Carilon Club in a thoughtful frame of mind. The talk with the Colonel had been very interesting.

Cassey, who was up north, was likely to prove a second Bilton, and Burke didn't worry about him at that moment. But it was of more than passing interest that Nathaniel Smethwick wasn't 'quite'. That could mean a great number of things, but the inference from Bilton's talk was that Smethwick didn't spend much time at the London office. Karen ruled the roost. And when he was out, the old dodderer Cuthbertson usually pestered Bilton's life, talking through his beard as he did so.

Jim Burke was highly suspicious of the Karen-Cuthbertson combination.

'I'll trot over,' he told himself, 'and ask for Smethwick. Smethwick won't be there.'

The London office of the steel goods firm that, in a time of considerable depression, was paying twenty-six per cent, proved to be a three-roomed suite in a one-eyed building in Cannon Street. A young clerk told him that Mr. Smethwick wasn't in, and would he like to see Mr. Cuthbertson?

'Please,' said Burke, and was ushered into the inner office, to find it very well furnished, as befitted the home of directors.

Mr. Cuthbertson, complete with brown beard, was standing by the window. He turned to welcome Burke, who had given his name as Martin, and for a moment Burke saw his eyes glitter behind thin, rimless glasses, and fancied the mouth, beneath that bushy brown beard, contracted. But Cuthbertson recovered himself quickly.

He stretched forth his hand in good Yorkshire fellowship, and his rosy cheeks were beaming.

'Mr. Martin? I haven't the pleasure of your acquaintance, but I'm glad to see you. What can I do for you?'

Burke murmured as if to himself.

'No, I don't think I will.'

Cuthbertson looked staggered.

'Will what, sir?' His voice was thick.

Burke smiled.

'Pull it off,' he said. 'The beard. It might hurt you, Adolf, and I wouldn't like to do that.'

Just for a moment Burke thought the other man was going to bluster a denial. But Adolf Karen changed his mind.

'So—you've found me,' he said heavily.

Burke helped himself to a chair and a cigarette.

'Yes, I've found you. I wouldn't move your hand pocketwards if I were you. I'm quick on the draw, and you're not likely to pull anything off with a gun if you fail with a tommy.'

Karen slumped into a chair, keeping his hands in sight.

'Not feeling chatty?' murmured Burke. 'A pity. I was hoping to get the inner history of the Daimler saloons and your dumb crowd of sharp-shooters, Adolf. Did it ever occur to you that you're not an overwhelming success as a gangster?'

Karen's beard drooped. He appeared to be considering the possibility of getting the better of the big man opposite him, though his chances in that respect were very thin. Actually, Karen was wondering whether the police knew too—if they came it would be the finish.

He licked his lips.

'You're lucky I'm not working for Craigie, aren't you?'

Karen swallowed hard, but said nothing.

'Because,' persisted Burke, 'if I was, I'd have had the police round here, and you'd have been taking your first step towards the gallows. A much nicer place, Adolf, to hear about than to visit.'

The big man paused, and regarded the relief in his victim's eyes. Karen found his tongue.

'If you're not with Craigie, who are you working for?' he muttered.

'Walk into my parlour, said the gangster to the spy.' Burke shook his head. 'That wasn't worthy of you, but I'll tell you that I'm working for certain'—he paused, then rolled the word out—'interests.'

'Interests?' Karen echoed the word.

Burke nodded.

'You got it, first time,' he congratulated. 'I can enlarge, Adolf, and say Big Business Interests. Interests worth a lot more money than—er—you.'

Karen leaned forward a little. There was a hungry look in his eyes, an expression that Burke knew well.

'Are you interested,' he demanded casually, 'in interests? Or do you prefer capital, Adolf?'

'Are you trying to bribe me?'

Burke waved his hands protestingly.

'What an idea! No, Adolf, I'm merely putting a theory to you. If—or shall we say supposing?—you were offered sufficient capital, would you impart any desired information about the connection between the firm of Smethwick and Karen and Marius Krotz? Nothing in writing, you know. Just a birdy whisper in the ear?'

Karen drummed nervously on his desk.

'What about the other things?'

'Other things?'

'The absurd idea'—Karen actually smiled—'that I am in some way connected with shooting affrays. Would you persist in that?'

'Why, no,' said Burke, shocked.

Karen hesitated and moistened his lips. Burke felt disgust for the man, yet if he offered a sufficient bribe, Karen would tell all he knew. It might be worth while to find the money, for the quicker the Krotz game was stopped the better. Burke, for all the zest of these activities, was not fool enough to want to drag them further than expediency demanded.

He was sure, in his own mind, that Karen could tell a story that would make his, and Craigie's job, simple, and he was equally sure that Karen would squeal.

It was a sudden glint in Karen's light blue eyes that warned him.

The glint came a fraction of a second before the hole that leapt into Karen's forehead, so Burke didn't see the blood ooze out. But he heard the zutt! of a silenced automatic behind him and almost on the instant he leapt from his chair and kicked it backwards!

The chair cracked against flesh and bone. A bullet buried itself in the carpet by Burke's feet and a second followed it. Burke crashed to the floor, unbalanced. Out of the corner of his eye he saw the clerk reeling back against the door, one knee bent, where the chair had caught him. His automatic was on the floor, a yard in front of him.

Burke's hand went to his pocket.

The clerk swore, his face twisted in fury, grabbed the chair and hurled it at Burke. Burke ducked, but the leg caught his shoulder, hampering his draw. The clerk stepped back into the passage, slamming the door. A key turned. Footsteps echoed down the stone steps of the building.

Burke scrambled up, hurried to the door and fired twice at the lock. The door sagged open. Burke pulled it wider and jumped into the outer office, but a wide-eyed typist, shivering with fright, impeded him. For the second time he went down, and as he went his head caught against the corner of the girl's desk. His head whirled. He closed his eyes as he hit the floor, and moaned a little.

Downstairs, a bare-headed youth flung himself into a taxi, snapping:

'Victoria Station. God, my knee!'

When the taxi-driver reached Victoria Station, however, no one got out of the cab. Remembering that 'my knee!' the cabby twisted his face into an expression of sympathy, and opened the door.

He stared into an empty cab, and then he cursed as he looked at the meter, with its four-shilling register.

Exactly two hours later, however, after interviewing a certain Dusty Miller at the Yard—most regular drivers knew Superintendent Miller—and a big man who sprawled over Miller's desk, he felt better. For despite the fact that he could only give his negative information he left the Yard with a pound in his pocket.

Burke looked at Miller as the door closed.

'I call that tough. Damn it, that clerk didn't look more than twenty. My, but they're a deep crowd, Miller. They had a spy planted at the London office, to watch Karen.'

Miller shrugged.

'So Karen wasn't the leader.'

'I'm hoping to find out a lot more about Adolf Karen,' said Burke, 'when we've searched that office thoroughly. Coming?'

Miller nodded.

Huddled in a greatcoat, the Superintendent looked the biggest man in London. Moving side by side they made an impressive pair as they hurried down the Yard steps to the waiting Squad car. They reached the Cannon Street office in fifteen minutes, just thirty seconds too late.

Things happened, as they had happened in the Krotz affair from the very beginning, with a kaleidoscopic swiftness. One moment the Squad car drew up outside the building, the next a man in a taxi with its hood down stood up and hurled something dark and round towards the open window of the private office of Smethwick and Karen Limited. A thin tail of smoke followed the thing, but Burke didn't look at it for long.

He bellowed into the driver's ear:

'Get after that cab!'

The car swung into the road. Miller sat down, hard, and with a curse. The cab was forty yards away, humming towards London Bridge.

Burke didn't see the passenger falling, but he did see the car swerve suddenly and heard it crash against a shop window. Almost simultaneously the roar came from behind them, and the office of the steelmakers bulged outwards and then rained, in large and small pieces, on the heads of the terrified passers-by.

11

A SURPRISE MEETING

Bedlam was let loose in Cannon Street, yet Burke heard nothing of it, beyond a vague, distant hum. Brakes were screeching, women and girls screaming, men and boys shouting, whistles shrilling. Like ants after honey the crowds streamed towards the scene of the crash and the explosion.

Solid and imperturbable policemen were forcing the crowd back from the smashed taxi, but let Miller and Burke through. The driver of the cab was crushed out of all recognition, but the passenger was moaning and groaning, trapped by a broken and torn seat. He was a dark-featured man, with sharp, ferrety features and lank black hair. A piece of his scalp had been taken off, and his right arm was crushed.

Burke turned to Miller.

'Get him to the nearest hospital, will you?' he said, 'and put two or three men in the ambulance and in the ward. A private ward. He might live to talk.'

Miller nodded.

Burke said, 'I'm going to look at the damage down in the office.'

'Be careful,' Miller said.

Burke nodded, lit a cigarette and hurried back to the scene of the explosion. His size enabled him to push through the seething crowd until he reached the unyielding wall of policemen. A sergeant said:

'Sorry, sir. No one's allowed past. Danger of fire.'

'All the more reason why I should get past,' said Burke.

'Sorry, sir.' The sergeant tugged at his walrus moustache.

Burke cursed the need for delay. It meant getting back to Miller and asking for an O.K. He turned, as a tall man in navy blue came up. The man looked at Burke and smiled. Burke didn't know him, but he blessed him as he said:

'All right, Coles. He can go through.'

'Thanks,' said Burke. 'But I don't know you.'

The plain-clothes man smiled.

'I'm detailed on your job, sir. And it's a pretty hard one, from what I can see.'

Burke shrugged his shoulders as they passed the impressed sergeant and hurried into the building. The office of Smethwick and Karen was on the second floor, but the effect of the explosion was visible on the first. Odds and ends of furniture littered the stairs; and something worse. A small, white hand, with a gaudy ring covered with blood, lay against the wall.

'Pretty grim,' muttered the detective.

Burke felt a fierce anger welling up inside him against the men who had done this thing. For the two girl typists in the office had been blown to bits.

The walls and partitions of the office were down, and a tongue of flame was licking along a wooden rail. Smoke and dust made it almost impossible to see the debris on the floor, but the thing Burke was after looked intact. It was a small steel safe, lying in a corner, door downwards. With the help of the detective and a plain-clothes man nearby, they turned it over, and Burke bit his lips in disappointment. The papers had been blown from it; obviously the door had been unlocked and thrown open by the force of the explosion.

'What are you after?' asked the detective.

'Papers of all and any kinds,' said Burke.

As the search of the ruined offices continued he realised more fully the damage. Two policemen who had been watching the office, after the shooting affray two hours or so before, had been badly injured. Both the girls, he confirmed, were dead—instantaneously, thank God! Firemen, summoned hurriedly, had little difficulty in quelling the flames, and the dust and smoke were thickened by the vile-smelling chemicals from the extinguishers. Through it all, Burke and his new-found friend searched grimly, but with little reward. Odd scraps of papers were found, but two or three small fires had destroyed most of the documents, apart from a steel file of records in the outer office which had escaped without damage. By some freak of the explosion a papier-mâché case, filled with oddments of feminine toilet, a bundle of paste sandwiches and a thermos flask of tea, was untouched.

Just an hour later Burke reached Whitehall and went by that circuitous route to Craigie's office. Craigie was looking grim.

'You've heard?' Burke dropped wearily into a chair.

Craigie nodded.

Burke pushed his hand through his hair.

'I ought to have expected something of the kind.'

'Steady,' murmured Craigie, who had seen that look of desperate, self-reproach in the eyes of other men.

'But it's true,' muttered Burke. 'I ought to have cleared the office before I chased after the taxi driver. And I ought to have searched the place, too. We would have found something, they wouldn't have chucked the bomb if there'd been nothing worth seeing.'

'Things like that have happened before,' said Craigie quietly. 'You've got to miss something, sooner or later.'

'I shouldn't have missed that,' growled Burke.

Craigie stood up, took a whisky bottle from the cupboard let in the wall next to the fireplace, and mixed a mild drink for himself and a stiff one for Burke. Burke pushed his hand through his hair, and a glimmer of a smile crossed his face.

'I suppose it's no use looking back,' he agreed. 'Have you found anything?'

'I had a message from the Westland hospital,' said Craigie. 'The man who threw the bomb from the taxi was Rogers.'

'The man who followed Carruthers the other night?'

'Yes.'

'So'—Burke lit a cigarette—'Karen wasn't vitally important. He was replaced immediately, or someone above him was watching all the time.'

'The latter, I fancy,' said the Chief of Department Z.

'That suggests that Karen's activities have been watched as closely as ours,' Burke said. 'Krotz has been doubling all his work.'

'Krotz never trusts any man,' said Craigie very slowly.

'We can estimate that Karen was working with at least seven others, which means a minimum of twenty agents are working in England. We've got to face that.'

Burke was quiet for a moment. Then his grey eyes burned into Craigie's.

'Am I doing well enough?' he asked simply. 'If you'd like to replace me, now's the time.'

'My dear chap,' said Craigie quietly. 'I couldn't.'

For the first time for many years a flush of embarrassment darkened Jim Burke's face, and Craigie went on hurriedly :

'Did you get anything before you went to Cannon Street?'

Burke recounted his talk with Colonel Bilton, his opinion that Bilton and Cassey were unimportant, but that the 'not quite'-ness of Nathaniel Smethwick might be interesting.

'Smethwick lives at Hampstead,' said Craigie. 'A house called Castleton, in Heath Road. Will you look it up, or shall I send someone else?'

'I'll go,' said Burke. 'But I could do with a couple of men, Gordon. The Arrans, if they're free.'

Craigie smiled a little.

'I'll fix you up,' he said, 'but not with the Arrans. They're trying to get on with a smattering of the Lathian language.'

Burke's eyes glinted.

'You mean they're in Lathia?'

'In Rikka,' said Gordon Craigie. 'I ought to get a report, from them, any time.'

It was six o'clock when Burke left the office and made for the Carilon Club where two agents of Z Department would meet him. He telephoned Carruthers as soon as he reached the club and found that young man in a depressed frame of mind.

'When will you be up and about?' asked Burke.

'Day after tomorrow,' Carruthers said glumly, 'and by that time everything will be over.'

'I wish you were right,' said Burke. 'I'll drop in tonight, if I'm still kicking.' He hesitated. 'Meanwhile I've a little job for you.'

Carruthers became more cheerful.

'Good man,' he said. 'Put it across.'

'You'll get a packet of papers,' said Burke, 'torn, burned, and generally messed about. I want you to try and piece as many together as possible; try and make some kind of sense out of 'em.'

'Anything for the cause,' said Carruthers.

Burke hung up and immediately called Miller, who was back at the Yard. The man Rogers, at the Westland hospital, was unconscious, and he had said nothing.

'Can't be helped,' Burke grunted. 'Miller, those odds and ends of papers you collected from the Cannon Street mess . . .'

'Yes?'

'Let Carruthers have 'em, will you?'

Carruthers being assured of getting the papers, Burke made for the grill room. It was early, and only half a dozen men were at the tables. Burke wasn't sorry. He chose a corner table, ordered a mixed grill, and contemplated the affair of Krotz from the beginning.

His contemplation had lasted less than five minutes before a waiter deposited a tankard, full and foaming, in front of him. Burke looked puzzled.

'I didn't . . .' he began.

'You're a perishing old liar,' said a genial voice from behind him. 'You did order it, Jim, and you're going to drink it.'

Burke regarded the ugly but homely face of a certain Robert Curtis without enthusiasm.

'So it was you, was it?'

'Why,' said Bob Curtis, admiringly, 'he guessed it, Wally. He's getting on.' Unasked, Curtis levered two chairs and drew one up to the table, leaving his companion, a leanfaced, tired-looking man, named Wallace Davidson, to do the same. He regarded Burke jovially.

'How's the life, old boy? Merry and bright?'

'It was,' said Burke pointedly.

'And now he's trying to be funny,' said Curtis, beaming at Davidson.

Burke resigned himself to the inevitable. He knew Curtis, who was probably the best-known man in a London set full of well-known people, and if there were times when he would have delighted in his company, this was certainly not one. Curtis was a powerful man, as tall as Burke himself, ugly, and possessed of a pair of roguish brown eyes and curly brown hair. He had money and spent it. During the summer he played a great deal of cricket, and during the winter hurled himself about the rugby field.

Davidson satisfied himself with swimming, rowing and tennis, and at none of these things was he more than an enthusiastic hopeful. He was a friendly but tired soul.

Curtis produced cigarettes.

'Lots of bright business about the old place, just lately,' he said chattily. 'Was I mistaken or was I not, when I hear you crashed in Kingston, James?'

'Ah,' said Burke, lifting his tankard. 'Here's to your good guess.'

Curtis chatted on, until Burke's grill arrived, and then he looked envious and thoughtful.

'No chance of shouldering in, I suppose,' he said, after a pause.

Burke looked at Curtis, and then, with a sigh, dipped his hand into his pocket for his wallet.

'I wondered what your trouble was,' he said wearily. 'Will a fiver see you through?'

Curtis accepted a fiver cheerfully, folded it and put it in his wallet, while handing a sheet of folded paper in return.

'Take that as security,' he said generously.

Burke might have tucked the paper away without looking at it, but for a peculiar glint in Curtis' eyes.

It was a code-letter on business heading, from Gordon Craigie. And it introduced Robert Montgomery Curtis and Wallace Davidson as Agents 17 and 21 of Department Z.

* * *

The house called Castleton, in Heath Road, Hampstead, was one of the older residences in that salubrious neighbourhood, and it was a solid, unpretentious building of red bricks and grey stone, standing in about an acre of well-kept garden.

Burke had decided that in visiting Nathaniel Smethwick he could safely describe himself as a police agent coming to discuss the outrage in the London office.

He had asked Craigie for help because he felt that the future activities would be fraught with more than usual danger, and a lone hand was inviting trouble. The lid was right off now, and the fighting wouldn't cease until one side or the other had won.

Davidson accompanied him to the house, while Bob Curtis sat at the wheel of a Rolls outside. None of them were expecting to meet trouble at Castleton, but all three were prepared for emergency.

Burke knocked on the heavy iron knocker. After a short pause, footsteps echoed inside the house. A hard-faced woman, dressed in servant's black, opened the door and stared uncompromisingly at the callers.

'Mr. Smethwick?' asked Burke pleasantly.

'Not seeing anyone,' snapped the woman.

'Now that's a pity,' said Burke, realising that soft-soap would be of little use.

'Kindly remove your foot,' snapped the woman coldly, 'and learn to take no for an answer, young man.'

'Well,' said Burke, gazing with astonishment at his foot, which was jammed against the door. 'Fancy that.' His voice hardened. 'Tell Mr. Smethwick that two police officers want to see him. And hurry.'

The woman's thin face relaxed. Burke was prepared to swear that she looked frightened. Then:

'But he's ill, sir.'

'I know,' said Burke. 'He's not too ill to see us.'

He walked past the servant into a square and drably furnished hall. Davidson followed him. The woman pointed to a settee.

'I'll see him,' she said grudgingly.

Burke grinned at Davidson as her straight back turned on them. Mr. Smethwick's housekeeper—he assumed—was not a sunshine lady. Nor did the furnishing of the hall suggest that its owner was managing director of a prominent steel firm which had shown substantial profits on the year's trading. And then he wondered how much was due to Smethwick, and how much its dreariness owed to the tightlipped woman.

A door opened, leading from a room at the front of the house to the hall. The housekeeper had gone up the narrow stairs, and Burke wondered whether Smethwick himself would appear.

The tall, distinguished-looking grey-haired man who entered the hall paused for a moment, and then stood stock still.

'Well,' murmured Burke, smiling frostily, 'if it isn't Mr. Hemming!'

Mr. Bart Hemming, American and friend of Patricia Carris, recovered quickly from his surprise, and advanced slowly, smiling easily and with calm assurance into the grim face of the big man.

Wally Davidson widened his eyes, looked wise, and looked on.

1 2

INCIDENT IN RIKKA

Timothy Arran, wrapped in three coats and two woollen scarves, poked his patrician nose above one of the latter. The nose was blue, his fingers were like sticks of ice, and his feet were frozen. He regarded a swelling, sleety grey sea for ten minutes from the deck of a cargo steamer, and eventually turned to his brother, who was standing immobile a yard away from him.

'It's cold,' said Tim, weightily.

'How bright you are!' said Toby, caustically. 'Why the hell we had to finish on this damned tramp beats me.'

'Safer,' murmured Tim.

'Can't see it,' grumbled Toby.

He was being cussed for the sake of it. He knew perfectly well that the journey to Lathia, which had been made mainly by aeroplane to the neighbouring country of Lithuania, and was being finished on the deck of the tramp, would have been useless if Krotz had discovered them, and there was little doubt that Krotz was watching all the airports.

The ship ploughed through the heavy seas, lurching wildly

and making the twins thankful they were good sailors. Through the grey mist, Rikka gradually appeared, a huddled-looking collection of dingy buildings and wharves. The ship docked and the Arrans passed through Customs, with their passports in good order and a declaration that they were brothers named Hopkins, travelling agents for a cotton manu-facturer. They hurried in a surprisingly up-to-date cab to a middle-class hotel in Konstrasse, one of the streets leading from the central thoroughfare of the Lathian capital, too cold to notice the tall, white buildings on either side, and the generally imposing appearance of Rikka's main streets.

Not until they were warming in front of a log fire in their bedroom, and were sipping hot punch brewed, according to the French manager, for all English guests, did they feel more human.

Timothy lit a cigarette.

'Well,' he said, 'we're here.'

By nine o'clock they were sufficiently warmed and well fed to view life more cheerfully. To make things better, a warm wind was blowing from the south, melting the snow that had filled the streets, making life considerably more pleasant.

Toby opened the window of the bedroom and looked out on the twinkling lights of Rikka.

'Better be moving,' he said.

'Try the manager again,' Tim answered.

The manager was only too pleased to do anything he could for the two English gentlemen. It appeared that they were hoping to visit a certain restaurant and cabaret, to which they had been recommended, but they could not remember the name of it.

The manager, a fat man with a pointed beard and mous-taches, beamed and understood.

'*Exactement.* Something to delight the eye, yes, and the

senses, no? Yes.' He considered. 'Eet ees the Ramplo Café, messieurs?'

Toby scratched his nose.

'That's not it, is it, Tim?'

'Doesn't sound right,' said Timothy.

The manager was desolate. 'But perhaps the Place Mikklen?'

Tim shook his head.

'Something like Dulin, or Dulen...'

'Ah-ha!' The manager lifted his hands in delight. 'But I am the fool, messieurs, not to have say it immediately, yes. The Café Dalinka, the finest, the brightest, the most ravishing café in all Rikka. Dalinka! Messieurs would like a guide?'

'Ah,' said Toby.

At twenty to ten they made their way towards the Briggas-trasse, the main thoroughfare, thankful for the rubber boots the manager had insisted on providing, walking through slush that was sometimes knee high. The vast, white buildings of Briggastrasse impressed even such experienced travellers as the Arrans. Rikka was a place worth seeing.

So, if the chattering guide at their side was anything to go by, was the Café Dalinka. The women! The music! The dances! It had to be seen to be believed.

'The gentlemen will like me to accompany them inside?'

'Be as well,' admitted Timothy.

They needed a guide, for their knowledge of the Lathian language was not of the highest, and for that evening at least they were anxious to do nothing that might arouse curiosity at the Dalinka. As they stopped outside a magnificent building gleaming with a thousand multi-coloured lights they told themselves that the Dalinka bore out all that was promised of it. Vast men in uniforms that would have shamed any field-marshal ushered them hither and thither, cloak-rooms,

English bar, American bar, Lathian bar. Soft-voiced waiters bowed about them, startlingly beautiful girl attendants hovered in and out of their sight.

Timothy regarded Toby with raised brows.

'Nifty.'

'Blinking marvel,' said Toby.

A princess in a shimmering gown of diamanté ogled them as they went, willingly, towards the fountain by which she was standing. A duchess in flaming red sidled up to them and pressed her fingers on Timothy's arm.

'Oh, ah!' said Timothy, grinning.

'No spik Lathian, sir?'

' 'Fraid not,' said Timothy.

'Me spik the Inglis excellent, yes. Sir, dance?'

Timothy looked at his brother and then at the vision in flaming red.

'All friends together,' he said.

The duchess frowned and pouted. Timothy was beginning to feel desperate when their guide, who had obviously prepared himself for the evening with the high spots, approached them, resplendent in evening dress. A babble of chatter and highly-coloured compliments ended in a round of smiles and the appearance of a countess attired in silver, who attached herself willingly to the guide. For an hour they danced, and the Arrans beamed brightly about them, two typical English travellers having an evening out.

The ballroom of the Dalinka was a huge, domed room, furnished with all the splendour of mid-European reckless-ness. Lights shone, wine sparkled, a dozen different tongues made Babel seem insignificant, dancing girls threaded between the tables, dancing couples changed partners almost with abandon.

'Is it always like this?' Tim asked the guide.

'But of course, m'sieu.'

'Mark it down for a peaceful trip, one day,' said Toby, *sotto voce.*

There would have been ample excuse if they had wished for different circumstances in their visit, for the Dalinka was like nothing they had ever experienced before. They had come from England, at Craigie's instigation, and they were to try and find an angle of the Krotz affair in the Lathian capital. Normally, of course, their chances would have been small, but they had Craigie's assurance that they would get a message at the Dalinka which would guide them on their movements. Craigie, with the shrewdness that characterised him, had stressed the fact that their visit was to be a flying one. They had just forty-eight hours in Rikka; after that they were to return to England, whether they had been successful or not. If, of course, a few additional hours would yield results, they would take them.

It was difficult to believe that any message could be given them in that hall of pleasure. Nothing but laughter and the cascading of wine seemed to matter. The pleasures of the Lathian upper class were obviously things of tremendous importance.

Timothy looked at his watch, and whistled. It was nearly two o'clock. No one seemed to think of going. If anything the Dalinka was fuller now than it had been at eleven. Tongues were a trifle looser, but the men carried their liquor well, Tim noticed. The music was certainly louder, coming from all corners of the great hall.

It stopped.

A few echoes of laughter rang through the silence. For a dreadful second Tim thought of trouble. And then the guide leaned towards him, his eyes gleaming with excitement.

'Messieurs are fortunate, yes! The King!'

His words rang in Tim's ears, to be drowned by the sudden crashing of the music from unseen orchestras. Everyone in the Dalinka jumped to their feet, craning their heads to see the entrance of that pleasure-loving gentleman, Frederik, King of Lathia.

Tim wrinkled his nose.

Frederik was dressed resplendently in uniform, and was walking straight ahead of him, inclining his head occasionally and very stiffly to the plaudits of the crowd. His nose was a beak, and his eyes were lewd, even at that distance. A weak chin and a thin, irritable mouth told Timothy and his twin that there was little to be said for the character of the Lathian king.

And then the guide's voice murmured into Tim's ear:

'And the great Krotz, m'sieu!'

Krotz!

Toby heard the whisper and the twins stared towards the royal party. There was no mistaking Krotz. He was the only one of the half-dozen sycophants in the little crowd dressed quietly and in English-cut evening dress. He was a big man, walking with considerably more presence than Frederik, but it was his face that held the attention. The U's of his forehead and his lips were more emphatic than ever, at that moment, his square chin was thrust forward, his black eyes glowed with inward pleasure, and roved about the hall. His bald head was like a pink skull-cap atop his swarthy skin and bushy brows.

The Arrans looked at Marius Krotz, and thought of Nick Carris.

The royal party moved slowly towards a raised dais at the end of the hall, and in front of it a hundred dancing girls whirled and sang.

Timothy dropped back in his chair and poured out a drink. Toby followed suit, saying he needed it. The guide turned excited eyes on them, and the duchess, the princess and the countess beamed with pleasure. The duchess, her shimmering red dress making Timothy blink at times, grew bold. She left her chair and shared Timothy's, putting a soft, white arm about his shoulder.

'Eet is so fine, sir, yes?'

'Hmm,' said Timothy, pondering. He looked at the girl's shining eyes, and patted her white hand. Her fingers tightened round his.

Toby, next to him, grinned slyly.

'Y'know,' began Timothy, disliking the prospect of calling the guide to his assistance. To make it worse, the Dalinka's patrons seemed to expect something of the sort.

'Y'know,' he started again.

Something harder than white flesh pressed against his hand. The duchess's eyes were still shining, her teeth gleaming against cherry red lips, but her hand, her fingers, were working into Timothy's, turning his palm upwards, working so slowly that she seemed to be caressing him all the time while actually slipping that piece of paper to him!

The duchess—*the message!*

Timothy swallowed hard, and played his part. His left hand toyed with the girl's hair, and he smiled cheerfully at her, while he buried the paper in his right palm and stealthily drew his hand away. He saw, too, that the countess was taking all their guide's attention. He unfolded the paper, holding it below the table, and glanced down quickly.

In very fine, black writing, was the message:

Leave immediately. I will meet you outside. We go to Krotz Villa.

Timothy pushed his hand through his hair, slipping the message into his mouth as he did so. A gulp of wine helped it down, for he knew that if all that caution had been necessary, the message had to be destroyed. There was a glint of approval in the duchess's eyes.

Timothy looked at Toby, his eyes flashing a message. Toby's eyes contracted a little. Tim fell across the table with a little gasp.

The guide stopped caressing the countess abruptly.

'M'sieu is not well?'

Timothy struggled to a sitting position. His half-closed eyes had a mistiness, and his lips sagged. He pushed his hand across his forehead, wearily.

'Hot,' he muttered. 'Must get out.'

The guide's disappointment was ludicrous.

'As m'sieu says . . .'

Toby rested a hand on the man's arm.

'You stay,' he said. 'Maybe we'll be back in a few minutes. All right?'

'But, m'sieu, my duty!'

Toby nodded, and winked deliberately at the countess, whose snow-white arms were enfolded round the guide's neck. The man beamed his gratitude.

'Come on, lad,' said Toby, giving his brother a helping hand. 'Keep your legs steady until we're out of here.'

Timothy grunted, and obeyed. They threaded their way through the tables, going by a long route to avoid passing the royal dais. It took them nearly ten minutes to reach the foyer where a host of commiserating nobility swept down on them. A doctor, a chemist, a strong drink?

'A spot of cold air,' said Toby, speaking to a huge man who spoke English well enough to understand him. The man nodded comprehendingly, and the twins' coats and hats were brought, Timothy was helped into his, money changed hands, and the Briggastrasse, with its white buildings and unending arc lamps, opened out before them.

They strolled slowly away from the Dalinka, towards Konstrasse and their hotel, keeping their eyes open and yet maintaining the pretence of Timothy's indisposition. Toby muttered:

'What was it?'

'The duchess,' muttered Timothy. He was just beginning to be surprised. 'Slipped a note in my hands. But I've got the idea.

'We're to go to Krotz's place,' he added quietly, 'Krotz is happy enough at the Dalinka for an hour or two, and we've time to look round.'

As he spoke, footsteps splashed in the mire behind them. Timothy caught a glimpse of two women, and recognised the duchess. They said nothing, but slackened their pace as the twins walked in their tracks. For perhaps twenty minutes all four went along the broad, straight streets, until they reached the fields beyond the city—the city, as Timothy said afterwards, without a suburb. Ahead of them a small building loomed out of the darkness. The two women entered it.

Timothy dropped his hand to his pocket and his automatic.

'God trusts him who trusts no one,' he murmured.

'Come on,' urged Toby.

They entered a small, square room, warmed by a log fire which supplied, also, the only illumination. The duchess appeared from the shadowy sides of the room, like a wraith.

'You did that very well,' she said, in flawless English.

Timothy swallowed hard.

'By hallelujah!' he said, 'and what about you?'

The girl laughed. Over her red evening frock she wore a

dark tailored coat, and the ends of the frock were tucked into rubber knee boots. Her accent was perfect and genuine.

'Yes,' she said. 'I am English. But we haven't much time. I had to wait until Krotz appeared. He's such a cunning beast, that you can't rely on reports. If he's at the Dalinka, though, with the King, he's all right for an hour or two. All the same, you'll have to hurry.'

A thousand questions hummed through Timothy's mind, but he didn't voice them. He was not used to the European work, and he realised that Department Z contacts in strange places and through strange people were spread throughout the continent. Moreover, each question he asked would take up valuable time. He nodded.

'What's the programme?'

The girl pointed towards a small, railed hole in the floor, on which the flickering light was shining vaguely.

'You go down there,' she said, 'and walk underground for about twenty yards. Then you'll find yourself in Krotz's grounds. You'll see the house, half a mile ahead of you. Go to the front door, and ask for Herra Marx.'

'Yes.'

'That's where our responsibility ends,' said the girl. 'Dee and I will stay here. If you have been followed—and most strangers are followed in Rikka—it'll be taken for granted you've come to see us.'

'Supposing someone looks in here, and finds us missing?' said Toby. 'You'll be for it.'

The girl laughed.

'You needn't worry about that,' she said. 'You get over to the Villa. And good luck.'

'Shall we see you again?'

'I don't know. In any case'—she rested a hand on each of the twins' arm—'don't worry about us. It's our job. Goodbye.'

The Arrans turned towards the hole in the floor. They were actually on the top step of a wooden ladder when something moved below. Timothy's eyes narrowed, and a gun sprang to his hand. A light was switched on in the underground passage, and the shadow of a man appeared. Two men . . .

Timothy drew back. Toby's gun was out, too.

The girl came to them, still smiling.

'They're all right,' she said. 'If anyone comes now, they'll take these two men for you. Don't worry. You're all right, until you've asked for Herra Marx.'

A light touch of her hand, and she was gone. The twins went downwards passing two men of a stature similar to their own and marvelling at the thoroughness with which this arrangement had been made. In silence they trudged on, finding the front door of the Villa in a straight line with the barn from which they had come. The house was large, impressive, somehow sinister. There was no sound, and only three lights shone.

Timothy was muttering under his breath. He was a fair linguist, and spoke German fluently; he would ask for the man Marx in German, and hope to be understood. Toby rapped the heavy knocker. The banging reverberated through the hall. No sound came, until the door opened with the slightest squeak.

A liveried flunkey bowed before them.

Timothy called on his German.

'You wish to see Herra Marx?' the flunkey repeated. 'You will wait, gentlemen?'

The twins stepped inside a tremendous hall, and walked towards the inevitable log fire, while the flunkey disappeared through a door by the side of a wide, oak staircase. There was a period of waiting that played on their nerves.

The door opened again, suddenly.

A short, square man, with a rather furtive air, hurried towards them. He held something that glittered, in his hand, and he thrust a bunch of keys into Tim's hand.

'Up the stairs,' he muttered, 'third door left, with red paint. Krotz's room. The safe's behind his bed. Marx isn't here, so don't worry. The flunkey'll be back in a minute. Hit him hard enough to finish him. Make sure of that.'

It was almost fantastic! This square-shouldered, furtive-looking Englishman standing in the great hall and muttering his words as if he was frightened of being overheard.

'All right,' said Tim.

The furtive Englishman disappeared. The door had hardly closed behind him when the flunkey came again, a man of medium height and with a pair of cruel, beady eyes.

'Herra Krotz and Herra Marx are not here,' he said. 'You have a message for him?'

'No,' said Timothy harshly.

The flunkey's hand dropped to his side. His eyes glittered.

'So!' he muttered. 'Spies?'

His gun flickered in the firelight, but before it was levelled Timothy had gripped the wrist in a vice-like hold and Toby had flung his hand over the man's mouth. The man squirmed wildly, desperately. Toby's hand sought his windpipe.

He got a grip.

'God!' he muttered, five minutes afterwards. 'Swinish. But I suppose it was him or us. Let's get to it.'

Through that tremendous hall and up the staircase they hurried, in a semi-darkness that was unnerving. The Villa Krotz seemed asleep. They hurried towards the red-painted door, the shadows thrown by the blazing log fire below them sending weird, fantastic shapes about the walls and eerie fears into their minds.

'Here,' muttered Toby at last.

The door opened. They found themselves in a bedroom large enough and luxurious enough for kings. A four-poster bed was set against the wall opposite a fireplace in which logs smouldered, and a dim light was spread through the chamber from a single wall-lamp. They hurried to the head of the bed, pulled aside the draperies and saw what they expected to see— the round face of a combination safe.

'Damn,' muttered Toby. 'The keys won't help.'

Timothy, strangely calm, looked hard at the metal and grunted.

'It's a false top,' he said. 'There's a keyhole there. Wait a minute.'

He worked quickly, but calmly, trying three keys before the first door opened. A second faced him, then a third. The minutes ticked by into eternity. The doors of the safe seemed unending, until Timothy muttered with satisfaction.

'Anything?' snapped Toby.

'Papers,' said Timothy. 'And a leather case. Two or three wall drawers, too. I'll get at them.'

It took him five minutes to strip the safe of everything it had contained. Then, cursing the delay, but realising the wisdom of it, he closed and relocked each door. All the time he tensed his ears, expecting almost at any minute to hear the clanging of an alarm. It was almost incredible that there was no system of burglar-alarms in the Villa Krotz. But it seemed true.

As he locked the last door, Toby finished distributing the papers and leather wallets about his person. They turned quickly towards the red door, breathing softly, hardly able to believe that they had succeeded in their mission.

Timothy opened the door.

'God,' he gasped, and the word seemed to echo inside him like a cold, stomach-turning shiver.

Toby's hand dropped like lightning to his gun, but the threatening muzzle of an automatic stopped him. In the hall stood a huge, bear-like man, with little black eyes hidden by tremendous bushy brows.

'So,' said Marx, and his eyes glittered.

13

KROTZ MOVES

They stood like statues, the two Englishmen barely reaching the Lathian's shoulder. The moment seemed eternity. Marx held the gun in a hand that dwarfed it, and they owed their lives to the fact that he was trying to remember if he had ever seen them before.

He was not over-gifted with brains, but he had learned certain rules while working for Marius Krotz, and he obeyed them with dog-like loyalty. In fact, a message had come from England to the steel and iron factory three miles outside the city, and he had hurried to the Villa immediately. He had tried the front door, found it locked, smashed a window and clambered into the villa, to find the flunkey dead in the hall. He knew what to expect when he reached Krotz's room—and he had found it.

Complete strangers.

Timothy suddenly fell backwards, and the bear-like brute did exactly what he expected—he fired where Timothy had been. The bullet hummed over Timothy's falling body, while Tim's feet kicked hard against Marx's knees. The man staggered. A second bullet smacked into the ceiling, but before a third came Timothy and Toby flung themselves at him.

It was like struggling with a bear. Marx heaved and snarled, whirling his great arms, forcing his elbow into Toby's mouth, kicking upwards, twisting, squirming, trying every trick. Toby tried for his gun, but the crushing weight of the man stopped him. Marx kicked suddenly against his stomach. Pain surged through him in vomiting fury. He dropped, gasping, trying to subdue the pain. Timothy was helpless in that great bear-hug. He pummelled the man's muscles, but might have been hitting cast-iron. Marx forced a huge hand round his throat. Timothy choked. A dying consciousness gave him one last hope, and he fumbled for his gun, but could not get it by the handle. With a last despairing effort he swung it, club fashion, into the brute's face. Steel succeeded where flesh and bone failed. Marx felt his nose smashed and dropped his victim, bellowing.

Timothy staggered against the door, taking in great gulps of air. His vision cleared as Marx, blood streaming from his nose, came again. The man was raging. He smashed his great fists towards Timothy, while the twin darted forward, bringing the gun down again on top of that hairy skull. Marx grunted. His eyes rolled. He thudded down, unconscious, and the landing shivered beneath his weight.

Timothy reeled backwards, hardly realising that the immediate danger was over. He stared stupidly at the huge bulk of the man and shuddered.

Toby had stopped moaning. Pain was still gripping his stomach, but he struggled up. A sickly grin crossed his face as he tugged at a small whisky flask in his hip pocket.

A swallow put new life into him. Timothy also drank, spluttered and took a deep breath.

'As near death as I've ever been,' he said.

Toby nodded, his face dead white.

'Let's get out,' he muttered.

They went down the stairs unsteadily. The front door opened at their touch and they went out, and the cold Baltic air whipped at their faces, refreshing them more than the whisky had done.

'Where?' asked Timothy.

'Try and find the girls,' muttered Toby.

They went through the front entrance of the Villa Krotz and picked up the trail of the path they had made across fields, a path made clear as the slush and snow had frozen again, in the cold night air. Fear lent them speed. The small black shape of the barn loomed ahead. Toby stumbled into the still-open exit of the tunnel through which they had hurried less than an hour before.

The heat of the barn made them gasp as they clambered up the wooden stairs. The fire was burning more brightly now. Vague shapes moved from the corners. The girl who had been the duchess in red hurried to them.

'Are you all right?'

'There'll be hell to pay,' muttered Timothy. 'We ran into a big brute.'

'Marx!' The girl uttered the name with a shudder. 'Well, you're safe here. That's the main thing. Where are the keys?'

Timothy handed them over unquestioningly.

'There's a motor-boat waiting, two miles from here,' the girl told him. 'We'll take you to it. You'll get across into Lithuania, you'll be all right there. Passports?'

'We're carrying them,' said Timothy.

The girl nodded. The two strange men went down into the tunnel again, to disappear for ever from the Arrans' ken. The girls wrapped themselves in coats, and left the barn with the Arrans at their heels.

'Hurry,' muttered the duchess. 'You'll have a beast of a journey tonight. It's freezing hard.'

'That's better,' said Toby, suddenly, 'than hell.'

The girls laughed. The Arrans lost all sense of values where courage was concerned, when they realised the risks these girls were taking, patrolling the ends of the earth, in effect, for a thin, hatchet-faced man in London who smoked a meerschaum for hour after hour. And in spite of the risks, they could laugh.

It took them half an hour to reach the cold, grey sea, ten minutes more to embark. Timothy stepped aboard last. His hand gripped the girl's whom he had called, a few hours before, the duchess.

'Can't you get away?' he said, almost pleadingly.

'We've a lot more to do,' she said. 'Goodbye and God speed.'

Timothy stepped into the small boat. The engine hummed and the nose cut through the icy sea. The figures of the women dropped out of sight, and the twins sat in the stern of the boat while a small, thin man, muffled up to his nose, forced every yard of speed out of his craft, driving for the three-mile limit and then Lithuania.

At half past two, while the revelries at the Dalinka were reaching a ribald climax, a powdered man in livery pushed his way towards the royal dais and caught the eye of Marius Krotz. A muttered conversation followed, before Krotz leaned towards Frederik.

'Urgent business takes me, sire,' said Krotz.

Frederik shrugged.

Krotz went off, forging a way through the crowd. A square-shouldered man with a furtive expression, but the features and appearance of an Englishman, was waiting nervously in the great foyer.

'Herra Krotz,' he muttered. 'Trouble at the villa. Marx has been hurt. Badly.'

The pupils of Krotz's eyes dilated as he walked quickly, but unhurriedly, to the waiting car. It was characteristic of him to say nothing throughout the short journey. Matthews, his English spy, might not have been there for s all the notice Krotz took of him.

Marx was conscious when he arrived. His nose was smashed beyond healing, and his skull was a mass of clotted blood. But his voice was as strong as ever.

Krotz listened intently until his servant finished. Then he went to the safe, opened it with keys from his own pocket, and saw the results of the burglary.

He swore coldly. His black eyes bored into Matthews'.

'Your keys,' he said very softly.

Matthews took the bunch from his pocket. Krotz looked at them and laughed suddenly.

'I suspected you,' he said.

'Herra Krotz!'

'If I thought there was any cause for it,' said Krotz evenly, 'I would slit your throat.'

Matthews said nothing. Krotz shrugged his shoulders.

'Now, Marx,' he said. 'You had a message at the factory?'

'But yes, Herra Krotz.' Marx took a cable from his pocket. Krotz read it, and he had no need this time to refer to the cypher. It ran:

Two Z men named Arran left in aeroplane for Northern Europe early this morning. 3.

'Arran,' Krotz mouthed the word. 'Matthews, do you know men named Arran?'

'But yes, Herra Krotz. They are Craigie's men.'

'That is certain?'

'As certain as anything can be.'

'So,' Krotz said. 'The men Arran left England this morning, arrived in Rikka this evening, came out here—were they two small men, Marx?'

'Yes, Herra Krotz.'

'Are the Arrans small men, Matthews?'

'Yes.'

'So they came out here, entering by asking for Marx, of whom they have probably never heard.'

'How can you tell that, Herra Krotz? Piet is dead.'

'Piet would have admitted no one unless they had asked for Marx. When I am out, no one enters unless they are messengers for Marx. So they asked for him, knowing he was not here, they killed Piet, opened the safe without keys, for only mine and yours are in existence, and escaped, while no alarm was raised. Remarkable, Matthews, that our alarm system failed?'

The furtive look in Matthews' eyes grew more pronounced.

'Inexplicable, Herra Krotz.'

Krotz smiled thinly.

'Marx, you have talked with the guard?'

'I have, Herra Krotz,' Marx growled. 'They were tricked into the grounds by rifle shooting, and locked in one of the sheds at the back.'

'Whoever arranged this is a clever man, eh, Marx?'

Marx spat.

'Eh, Matthews?'

'It is incomprehensible, Herra Krotz.'

'Is it?' asked Krotz slowly. He motioned to Marx, casually. 'Hold him, Marx.'

The man's great hands fixed themselves about Matthews' arms, forcing Matthews a foot forward, only a few inches from the cold, deadly face of Marius Krotz.

Krotz drew a knife from his pocket.

'I have cut throats,' he said, 'from ear to ear, Matthews. What would you think if I were to cut yours?'

Matthews' eyes lost their furtiveness. His shoulders squared. There was no chance of escape now. Every possible trick to keep suspicion away from him had been tried. The Arrans had come from England to commit a theft that he could have contrived himself, simply to try and ensure that Matthews was still allowed to work for Krotz, above suspicion. But the effort had failed.

The smile on his face was very calm.

'Well?' asked Krotz. The point of the knife drew blood from beneath Matthews' left ear.

'I should say,' said Matthews, very quietly, 'that you were several hours too late, Herra Krotz.'

There was a dead silence. Then the knife slashed round.

Krotz looked into the cruel eyes of his bear-like servant. It was nearly twenty minutes later, and there was no sign of blood on the carpet, no whisper of death in the air.

'And so,' said Krotz, 'I made the mistake of believing he could do no harm. A pity. He was useful. Now, we have a great deal of work.'

'We have, Herra Krotz.'

'We might have to act almost immediately, Marx. Have everything ready.'

'It will take two days, Herra Krotz.'

'That is all right. The aeroplanes will be ready first, you understand?'

'They are ready at any time, Herra Krotz.'

'You must go and get first aid,' said Marius Krotz.

The door closed behind the servant. Krotz stepped noiselessly to the window and looked across the slush-bound fields to the distant lights of the capital.

All his life he had fought for revolution, all his life he had hated monarchy. But he hated the established order of things even more.

But Marius Krotz had never hated anything sufficiently to forget himself. He needed help, and the help was waiting for him to call to action. Not Russia. He didn't trust Russia now. But there were nations that must expand.

'But it's too early,' muttered Krotz, to the twinkling lights of Rikka. 'If I can take those papers from the Arrans before Craigie gets them . . .'

He turned away, quickly, and reached for his telephone. Cables were useless, now. He wanted action quickly. The Arrans might be on the way to England, by air.

The Arrans were too cold to speak. They thought that a different means of transport might have been provided, but realised, dimly, that a bigger craft could not have got away from Rikka without being seen.

The boat raced on.

Two miles off shore, a blanket of fog swallowed them. They heard the sea swishing about them, and the man at the wheel swearing. He switched on a light that did no more than make the fog a lighter grey.

The wail of the siren, the clearing of the mist and the vast, immovable side of the oncoming steamer came almost at once. Before they had time to realise the meaning of that high-pitched wail, they saw the steel plates looming above them. The man at the wheel tried to turn, but it was too late.

The boat crashed against those merciless steel sides.

The steamer went on, its siren whining through the darkness, and the icy waters supported the unconscious Timothy, a Toby Arran who was gripping his brother's coat and cursing inwardly, and the wreckage of the launch. Its owner had split his head against the steel and Toby had seen him go down.

Toby Arran knew despair.

14

HEMMING MAKES MORE MYSTERY

The three men in the hall of Castleton, in Hampstead, regarded each other with varying expressions: a deliberate hostility in Jim Burke's eyes, a slightly amused and annoying tolerance in Hemmings', and uncertainty in Wally Davidson's, who knew nothing of the American.

'Well,' said Burke.

Hemming shrugged his shoulders. He wasn't so old as Burke had thought, despite his greying hair. He looked every whit as immaculate as he had at the Mayday Club, and at the station when Patricia had left for Scotland.

'This is something of a surprise, Burke,' he said, with the slightest American intonation.

'Something,' said Burke, 'is a mild word. You wouldn't like to tell me what you're doing here, would you?'

Hemming laughed.

'Can I ask you the same?'

'I'm on business,' Burke said. 'Official business, to do with a certain blow-out in Cannon Street.'

'That,' said Hemming, taking a cigarette case from his pocket. 'I see.'

'Are you going to talk?'

'I hadn't thought on those lines,' murmured Hemming.

'You can always change your mind,' said Burke, affably. 'Try and understand this. I'm here on official business and the affair in Cannon Street has to be solved. A suspect is a suspect.'

'You build suspicions pretty quickly,' said Hemming; there was a suggestion of anxiety in his eyes.

'I do a lot of things quickly,' said Burke.

'And you haven't yet convinced me that you're a police official.'

'I shouldn't let that little formality encourage you,' said Burke. 'What are you doing here?'

Hemming answered levelly enough.

'I've been talking with Smethwick.'

'What about?'

'Business.'

'What's the connection between fabric mills and steel-work?' demanded Burke.

'So you know that, do you?' murmured Hemming. 'Well, the connection isn't obvious, but I could call it financial.'

'You could also call it stronger things,' said Burke. 'I'm asking you what you came about.'

Hemming shrugged.

'We aren't going to get much further, this way,' he said. 'My business with Smethwick was quite genuine. That ought to suffice you.'

'Can you prove it?' asked Burke.

'You're an obstinate man,' Hemming said, 'but I wish you had a little more imagination.'

'Lots of people have wished that,' Burke said. 'Wally'—he

glanced at his companion—'I think Mr. Bartholomew Hemming wants a once-over.'

'Anything you like,' said Davidson. He moved a little wearily towards the American, but didn't touch him. With Burke, he saw the tensing of the man's muscles, and half expected violence. But Hemming controlled himself, and his voice was steady but cold.

'Be careful,' he said. 'American citizens have certain rights. I don't imagine you'd get away with anything.'

Burke's eyes widened.

'The police can always make a mistake,' he said, almost chidingly.

'And would the police admit anything about you?' asked Hemming. 'I always thought you worked at your own risk.'

'We're getting on,' Burke said. 'You know about the Cannon Street affair, you know I'm not on the regular police.'

'I assumed it,' replied Hemming.

'Good enough for me,' said Burke. 'Wally, I hope he doesn't make a fight of it. Fan him!'

Wally moved again.

Hemming, his eyes on Burke's right hand—or on the pocket that hid it—drew himself up as if in challenge. Wally's hand actually touched his coat before he whipped a hook towards the weary-looking man's chin. Davidson slipped it without trouble.

'You'll get hurt,' he warned.

Hemming looked ready to make a real fight of it when a door opened and the tight-lipped woman appeared. Her eyes glittered as she saw the trio, and she lifted her black skirt, too swiftly for indelicacy.

'What's all this?' she demanded.

The small gun in her bony hand could kill, Burke knew, and he was at a disadvantage. He doubted her sincerity, but he didn't want to take chances, just then. And in his mind there was a remarkable vision of a 'not quite' director whose house-keeper carried an automatic.

'Just a little chat,' he said, genially, 'and I shouldn't play with that. It might . . .'

'It will go off, if you're not careful,' warned the tight-lipped woman. 'Outrageous—entering a man's house and assaulting his visitors. Why don't you call the police, Mr. Hemming?'

Burke smiled at her, and kept his hand in his pocket.

'You've forgotten,' he murmured, 'that I *am* the police.'

The woman's eyes glittered.

'I don't believe it for a minute. You're forcing a way into this house under false pretences, and the law—ah!'

Burke didn't see Hemming's fist until it was an inch beneath his nose. It was a hard fist, and it thudded with all the power of thirteen stone of bone and muscle. Tears flooded the big man's eyes. He didn't see the left-arm hook that caught Wally Davidson in the stomach and sent that worthy gasping against the wall. Only dimly did he hear the door bang—the street door. It was fully two minutes before he had recovered sufficiently to think, by which time Wally was regarding the thin-lipped shrew whose eyes glinted with unspoken triumph.

'You shouldn't have let him do that,' said Wally, shaking his head admonishingly.

At another time Burke might have admired the gentleness of the reproach, but at that moment he was incapable of admiring anything, and his opinion of the tight-lipped servant was too strong for words. He ignored the woman and stepped to Davidson's side. The tired-looking man grinned and nodded before he went out of the house. Burke, grim-faced, regarded the woman.

'You're going to have another spell behind bars, for that,' he said.

There was a tense silence. The woman's lips twisted in a snarl, but there was fear in her eyes.

'What do you mean?' she muttered. 'I've never . . .'

'You have,' snapped Burke. 'And you're going to have a lot of trouble denying it. Drop that gun!'

She wavered. He saw her finger on the trigger, and no longer doubted her quality.

He fired through his pocket, spoiling a fourteen-guinea suit, a thirty-shilling black dress and a twenty-guinea carpet within a fraction of a second of each other. As the bullet tore through the folds of her skirt the woman dropped her gun, like a live thing. A bullet hummed from it, burying itself in the floor. Her eyes widened in fear.

'Don't!' she moaned, 'don't!'

Burke doubted whether he could have brought himself to shoot her, dangerous though she had been. But the crisis was past. He jerked his thumb towards a telephone.

'Call Scotland Yard.'

The woman hesitated.

'Call them!'

She obeyed. Burke directed her to ask for Superintendent Miller, and smiled as her voice quavered into the mouthpiece. He asked Miller, through her, to send a couple of reliable men to Castleton, and received Miller's assurance through the same medium. She was almost prostrate by the time she had finished. Burke was glad Davidson re-entered the hall, immediately afterwards.

'Has Bob gone?' asked Burke.

'Yes. Bucked to death.'

'He would be,' grinned Burke. 'Now watch this sweet maid for a few minutes, Wally, while I look round for the precious Nathaniel. A couple of men from the Yard will relieve you in a few minutes, and you can tell 'em just why you're holding her.'

'What then?' asked Davidson.

'Look round for me,' said Burke.

Burke searched the downstairs rooms, drawing blank, but discovering, in a room that looked out on a large back garden, a heap of burned papers in the grate. He sifted the papers, but found nothing of any use. He prepared to go back to the hall in order to reach the upstairs rooms, when an open door that appeared to lead to nowhere but a large cupboard caught his eye.

He went to the door—and then he whistled.

Mr. Nathaniel Smethwick had a lot of strange whims, it appeared.

For the cupboard was a small, electric lift, leading from the kitchen quarters to the rooms above. It was too large for a service lift, and in any case, it was not fitted with shelves. Obviously it was intended for passengers.

'And this Mr. Smethwick,' murmured Burke, stepping into the lift and pressing the control button, 'isn't "quite". Quite what, I wonder? And we've been letting this go for three whole days!'

The lift stopped, and he stepped into a large, airy bedroom, obviously one that had been used recently. He sniffed. Tobacco smoke was in the room. A tiny spiral of grey going upwards from a cigarette butt in the hearth caught his attention. He retrieved it, and saw at the end of the butt the gold letters:

'. . . panol.'

'Panol,' he said aloud. 'Don't recognise it, but it's probably Hemming's. I wonder where Smethwick is?'

He passed from the large bedroom to a smaller one, well-furnished but unoccupied. The door led into the passage at the head of the stairs, and looking downwards, he saw Wally resting wearily against the wall and regarding the woman with half-closed eyes.

They were all right.

There were four closed doors leading from the other side of the landing, and the first revealed a surprisingly large and luxurious bathroom. Burke noted these remarkable contrasts —the dowdy hall and the expensive bathroom, the ill-furnished downstairs rooms and the luxurious bedrooms—and then he sniffed again, at something very different from tobacco smoke.

'Damn,' he said. 'That's one thing we don't want.'

The sweet but slightly acrid smell of pines assailed his nostrils, mingling with something more delicate. He could conceive of a man bathing with pine salts, but he couldn't fix his mind to believe that a man would use the more perfumed toilet aid.

He peered into the porcelain bath. The slightest powder of undissolved salts was at the bottom, and when he touched the sides of the bath he felt them warmer at the bottom than at the top.

'Recently used,' he muttered. 'Surely the hag downstairs doesn't use bath salts . . .'

The thought amused him, as he opened the next door.

Peering forward, he felt his limbs go suddenly weak, and he leaned back for a moment against the wall.

Stretched out on the floor, partly covered by a bath wrap but with the white skin of her shoulders and arms gleaming beneath the electric light, which was full on, was a girl; a girl with blonde hair that drooped from her head to the floor. One lock of it was wet . . .

It was hanging in a pool of blood, blood that came from the throat of an old man who was lying on the floor next to the girl. His arms were stretched straight out, but his legs were bent beneath him—and his eyes, wide open, stared glassily towards the ceiling.

That man was dead.

Smethwick...

Burke saw a mental vision of a suave, immaculate American, and, even in the presence of death, he cursed that man coldly, deliberately.

15

A DISCOVER AT WEMBLEY

The girl was not dead.

As Burke made sure of that, he saw the ugly, red bruise on her forehead. Probably she had heard the old man call out, hurried into his room and been knocked unconscious.

There was an old settee against one wall of the room and he picked the girl up and carried her to it, covering her with the bath wrap and arranging his overcoat on top of it. Then he went to the head of the stairs. His eyes were hard; he was still thinking of Bartholomew Hemming.

Davidson was lounging against the front door. Burke was about to call, but stopped as footsteps sounded outside the house and a heavy knock echoed through the hall. Davidson opened the door quickly. The woman's eyes were narrowed and furtive. She was fearful that the newcomers were the police.

They were. Miller's burly frame appeared and two plain-clothes men followed him.

'Where's Burke?' asked Miller, nodding at Davidson.

'Here,' said Burke, from the head of the stairs. 'Come up, will you, and get one of your boys to call for a doctor. You'll want all the usual paraphernalia, too.'

Miller blinked.

'What is it?' he asked.

'Murder,' said Burke.

Miller rubbed his square jaw and turned to the nearest detective. Simultaneously the woman threw up her bony hands and screamed. The sound echoed through the house. Davidson moved towards her with unexpected speed.

'Stop it,' he said.

The woman screamed again. And then, while Davidson was reaching for her, she collapsed in a heap on the floor.

Miller, with typical dourness, was talking to his man and giving instructions, heedless of the din. The man turned to the phone as Burke called down.

'Better look for Bartholomew Hemming, Super.'

If Miller was surprised he didn't show it.

'Have you got enough on him to make a charge?' he demanded from the bottom stair.

'He was here twenty minutes ago,' said Burke. 'Smethwick's been dead for about half an hour, I'd say.'

Miller nodded, and gave further instructions.

'Tell them Hemming lives at the American Club,' he said. 'Dawson knows him by sight.'

The plain-clothes man was at the telephone by the time Miller reached the head of the stairs. Neither he nor Burke spoke as they hurried inside the room. Miller's lips moved silently. He bent over Smethwick, a pure formality, and then looked at the girl.

'What's her trouble?' he asked.

'She'll be awake in a minute,' said Burke.

'Know anything?' Miller, who was used to these things by

now, was patting his pockets for cigarettes. He was a chronic smoker of other people's cigarettes, and drinker of their whisky. Burke reported briefly what he had found since he had called at Castleton, and Miller listened attentively.

'Of course,' said Miller, cocking an eye, 'you're sure Smethwick was connected with Karen—apart from ordinary business, I mean?'

'It looks like it,' said Burke, motioning to the huddled figure of the old man.

Miller shrugged his shoulders, phlegmatically.

'Doesn't do to be sure,' he said, 'unless you know. Let's see. Supposing Smethwick was fooling with her'—he poked a spatulate thumb towards the unconscious girl—'and supposing she had a jealous husband.'

Burke was rubbing his chin slowly.

'It might not be connected with the Karen business?'

Miller nodded, and lit a cigarette.

'It isn't a typical Karen killing,' he said. 'Of course, it might be connected. But the other's a possibility.'

'The damned—clever—swine!' said Burke, very softly.

'Now if I hadn't seen Hemming here, if the discovery had been made in the usual way, it would have seemed . . .'

'A passion murder,' said Miller, who possessed a flowery imagination for a dour and apparently strong-minded man.

'Yes,' murmured Burke.

'And remember,' said Miller, walking towards the settee suddenly and looking hard into the girl's face, 'you can't be sure Hemming's connected. Can you? Or are you?'

Burke hesitated.

'No, I haven't any real reason for believing it,' he said. 'Not connected with the Karen business, I mean.'

'That's what I mean,' said Miller ruminatively. 'Seen this face before, somewhere,' he added. 'It wouldn't surprise me if we've got a record of her at the Yard.' He looked away from her and went towards the window, opening it, and poking his head into the cold night air. 'Of course, Hemming might not have done this...'

'You're being helpful,' said Burke.

'I'm just pointing it out,' Miller said. 'Hemming went out of the front door. It wouldn't be easy for anyone to get out of this window, but there's bound to be a rear exit. Still.'

'Anything more you want me for here?' Burke asked.

Miller stared reflectively.

'Don't think so. I'll look after the woman downstairs and this girl.'

'I'm not going before this girl wakes up,' said Burke. 'She might talk.' He rubbed his chin. 'Any reason why she's got to wake up and see this?'

'No,' said Miller. 'We can get all the pictures of Smethwick by himself. You haven't moved anything, you say?'

'No,' said Burke. 'Apart from shifting the girl to the couch.'

'And she wasn't touching Smethwick?' persisted Miller.

Burke frowned, but his voice was level.

'Her hair was wet with blood,' he said, 'but they weren't touching.'

Miller nodded. Burke walked to the window and looked out across the darkness of Hampstead Heath. He was more concerned, just then, with Miller's attitude than with anything else.

Burke wasn't a fool. He knew that Miller had been affable and friendly during the few days he had known him, and now he sensed a definite change in the policeman's manner. Miller was vaguely hostile. It was almost as if he was suspicious of Burke.

What had caused the change?

There was one possible reason, Burke knew, but he didn't

let himself think about it at that moment. But he was more relieved than he admitted even to himself when he heard a slight moan from the settee. He turned round quickly. The girl's eyes were opened. She closed them again quickly.

'Let's get her out of here,' said Burke.

Miller nodded, but made no attempt to help. Burke took the girl in his arms and went quickly towards the next bedroom. Miller followed close behind. The girl opened her eyes dazedly, and Burke smiled as he put her on the bed.

She laid her head back on the pillows, and her voice was very low.

'Did you find him?'

Burke nodded.

'Don't worry about it,' he said. 'Do you feel like talking?'

The girl's eyes were wide open now, and she glanced at Miller. Burke found her wan prettiness strangely moving. The darkening clot of blood in her hair was ugly.

'What happened?' asked Miller, his tone gentle enough. Whatever had affected his trust in Burke, it wasn't affecting his humanity.

The girl shuddered.

'I had just finished a bath when I heard him shout. So I threw a wrap round my shoulders and hurried . . .'

She stopped, closing her eyes, and the only spark of colour in her face was her red lips, Burke noticed.

'Well?' he prompted, very softly.

'He was lying there with a wound in his throat,' she said in a flat voice.

'Was there anyone else?'

She nodded.

'Yes. I didn't see him, though. I heard a sound behind me, and then something hit me.'

Miller was rubbing his chin, satisfied, it seemed, to let Burke ask the questions.

'And you didn't see anyone here at all?' Burke asked.

The girl's eyes met his squarely.

'Before I went into the bathroom, there was Mr. Wooderson.'

'What is he like?'

'A tall, grey-haired man. An American, I think, but I don't know. He's been here several times to talk with Mr. Smethwick.'

So Bartholomew Hemming was known to Smethwick by the name of Wooderson. Murderer, or not, Hemming had a lot of questions to answer.

'Where was Wooderson—or Hemming?' Burke persisted.

'Downstairs, in the front room, with Mr. Smethwick.'

She closed her eyes again. For the first time Burke took a flask from his hip pocket and moistened her lips with whisky. She coughed a little.

'Better?' he asked.

'Yes, thank you.'

'Half a minute,' said Miller, suddenly. 'Just stay here, Burke, will you. There's someone downstairs.'

Burke nodded, and watched the Super leave the room, still wondering what was worrying him. He heard the mutter of voices below the stairs and heard a car draw up. The Yard men, with their cameras and the usual impedimenta, he told himself.

Burke looked at the girl.

Her eyes were wide open now, and she was staring at him fixedly, almost in fear.

'What's the trouble?' asked Burke, very softly.

She hesitated. Her fingers fastened about his arm suddenly, with more strength than he expected.

Her voice was very low and tense.

'Are you *James* Burke?'

He nodded, wondering how she came to know.

'Get away,' she said suddenly, fiercely. 'Wembley. Grand Drive. It's a private hotel.'

Burke's fingers clenched.

He stared at the white, tense face of the girl, and he could hardly believe his ears. She *had* spoken. 'Get away from here. Wembley. Grand Drive . . .'

He hadn't time to think before footsteps echoed on the stairs, the heavy, deliberate tread of Horace Miller.

The girl's grip tightened on his arm.

'Don't tell the police,' she said, and her voice was like a prayer. *'Please!'*

Her slim body was raised from the bed, and he felt her quivering. Miller's steps drew nearer. She dropped back, and her eyes closed. Miller came in.

'All right,' he said. 'A doctor'll have a look at her in a moment. Better let her rest for a while.'

Burke nodded.

'I don't think we'll get much more from her,' he said. 'I think I'll be getting along.'

'Please yourself,' said Miller.

Burke nodded to the girl and walked into the passage.

Davidson was waiting in the hall, watching a young army of plain-clothes men invade the house. Two of them walked past Burke as he reached the bottom stair, and he saw that they were carrying a camera and tripod. The helpful detective who had enabled Burke to get past the police cordon round the Cannon Street office of Smethwick and Karen was there. Burke smiled at him. The man nodded, curtly. There was no trace of friendliness.

'Wally, we're moving,' he said.

He wouldn't have been surprised if there had been trouble about leaving Castleton, but the detective stood aside, and the two Department men walked into Heath Drive.

'I've seen Miller before,' said Davidson, 'but I've never seen him freeze up like he did tonight. Notice it?'

'I've upset him, somehow,' Burke said. 'But that's by the way. We've got to get to Wembley, and in a hurry.'

Davidson lengthened his stride. It was a big point in his favour that he accepted all orders with complete acquiescence.

'Going by train?' he asked.

'No,' said Burke. 'I'm going to hire a car, if I can, or find a cab. While I'm bargaining, you can call Craigie. Know his number?'

'Yes.'

'Tell him we're going to a private hotel in Grand Drive, Wembley,' he said, 'and tell him Smethwick's been murdered, and Hemming's involved somewhere.'

'Hm-hm,' said Davidson.

They reached the Heath Station and Davidson hurried to a call-box while Burke looked round for a garage where he might be able to hire a car. Twenty yards further up the road from the station, the lights of a petrol pump flared against the night. Burke hurried towards them.

Five minutes later Wally Davidson stepped out of the call-box, frowning and scratching his head. He didn't know Burke particularly well, but he liked what he did know of him. And he couldn't understand the message Craigie had given him; at least, he couldn't understand the reason for it.

For Craigie had said:

'Tell Burke I want to see him before he goes anywhere. And make him come, Davidson.'

And make him come!

Davidson hurried towards the garage and felt the gun in his pocket.

Was Burke likely to object? Davidson hoped not, but he was prepared to use force, or the threat of force, and the size of Jim Burke didn't worry him.

Or it wouldn't have worried him, if he had been there.

For another five minutes Davidson paced up and down the road, and finally he made enquiries at the garage. Yes, a big man had hired a car, the fastest car in the garage, a Lancia, and had driven off with a speed that made the garage proprietor glad he'd been paid a substantial deposit in hard cash.

Davidson walked quickly back to the telephone booth. Craigie had to know about this at once.

At nine o'clock on that bleak March evening a long-nosed Lancia tourer swung off the Wembley-Harlesden road, and climbed the slight rise that led to Grand Drive.

Burke was feeling grim. The Drive was one of the turnings to the right, just before the road that led past the Exhibition grounds. The houses were a good, residential kind.

Halfway along the road was a house larger than its immediate neighbours and possessing more extensive grounds that looked unkempt even in the gloom. The garden didn't interest Burke, but the weather-beaten sign, stuck between two posts at the front of the garden, did.

He drove the Lancia a dozen yards further along, stopped it, climbed out and walked swiftly back to the house with the sign, which ran:

The Drive Private Hotel

Beneath it, in still smaller printing, was the information that it was well recommended.

Burke lit a cigarette, felt his gun, and opened the small gate leading to the front door of the private hotel.

It had never been his habit to hesitate for long, and he had done all the thinking he needed during the run from Hampstead. Burke possessed a savage, inward anger at the way things had developed—but in a cooler frame of mind he would have admitted there was considerable justification for them.

He hadn't known Craigie's message to Davidson, of course, but he had sent that gentleman to contact with Craigie while he looked for the car, half expecting Craigie's reaction. Craigie might well be poisoned with the same doubt as Horace Miller, and although Craigie would have revealed it differently, it did not mean that his actions would be substantially different. It would have meant delay, and Burke did not want delay.

He might have faced it but for the message from the girl. At Castleton, he had been turning over in his mind the wisdom of going straight to Craigie and asking whether the Chief knew the reason for Miller's face-about. But the girl had changed things.

She may have urged him to go to Wembley to trick him, of course. Most suspicious-minded men would have assumed that, and taken strong precautions. But Burke thought it well worth taking a chance.

First, the girl had been knocked out, which suggested she wouldn't be well-disposed to whoever had struck her. Second, she had had no time to speak or consult anyone, after recovering consciousness. Both of those things suggested that she had been obeying an impulse when she spoke to Burke. Then he remembered the change that had come over her when she had heard Miller call him by name. This, together with her obvious anxiety to keep the thing away from the police, heightened the impression of impulsiveness.

And stronger perhaps than any of these things was the fact that he had seen her wan, pale face on the pillows.

At last he knocked on the front door of the private hotel in Grand Drive.

There was no response, until he knocked again, and then the sharp sound of leather-heeled shoes striking solid wood flooring came to his ears. The steps were long ones, he judged those of a man.

He waited, with his right hand fondling the butt of the gun in his pocket.

The sound of a bolt being drawn came next, then the clinking of a small chain. The proprietors of the hotel took unusual precautions, for that time of night. Burke waited, as the door began to open.

A massive man stood framed in the doorway, his burly figure a silhouette against the light from a room at the end of a long passage. The man's hand was in his pocket. His face was swarthy and unpleasant, even when he peered through the gloom at the caller.

Then it was distorted—vicious, murderous.

Two shots stabbed through the semi-darkness, almost simultaneously. A bullet tore through Burke's overcoat and dropped on to the path beyond. The man in the door yelped, and clutched at his shoulder, dropping his gun. It clattered on the stone steps as Burke jumped into the hall, pushing the other before him, and slammed the door.

Then he looked into the livid face of Gustav Hermann, servant of Adolf Karen and the man who had once held Burke and Carruthers up in the hall of Longtree House!

16

TROUBLE AT WEMBLEY

Burke didn't trouble to tell himself that the girl at Hampstead had tricked him. In point of fact, he didn't stop to consider anything but the fact that he had Hermann here, against the wall.

He stared grimly at the man.

Hermann said nothing. He was clutching at his shoulder and blood was streaming between his fingers. Burke knew he wasn't badly hurt, however; the thing that worried Hermann was the sight of his gun. Burke raised it. Hermann drew back.

He didn't see Burke twist the gun round, but he felt the butt thud against his head; and then he groaned, and slumped down. Burke dropped his automatic into his pocket, took out a handkerchief and, pulling the unconscious man's wrists together, bound them quickly. Then he stripped the tie from Hermann's collar, and used it to secure his legs.

The light from the room at the end of the passage enabled him to see well enough. There was no sound in the house. The silence puzzled and yet cheered him. He had forgotten everything, now.

A door leading to one of the front rooms was partly open. Burke went in, and switched on the light. It was empty, and furnished as a lounge, large enough to hold a dozen people comfortably. Burke went back into the passage, lugged Hermann along the polished floor into the room. There was no key in the lock, but Hermann was likely to be unconscious for ten minutes or so, and helpless for an hour after that.

Burke closed the door and went back to the lighted room.

The first sound he had heard since Hermann had let his teeth chatter came suddenly and with exaggerated volume through the silence. A shuffle of footsteps at the end of the passage.

Burke took his gun and went forward.

An untidy figure of a man moved into sight, a man who was looking at his toes until Burke's 'keep very still' broke through the near-silence. The man started.

'Well,' murmured Burke, 'we are meeting a lot of old friends tonight.'

'I . . .' began the other man.

'Very quiet, I said,' murmured Burke.

He advanced into the room, and the man backed away from him, a stocky Cockney dressed in navy blue, and who went by the name of Carter. The man, in short, who had been followed halfway across London on the evening when Carruthers had nearly met his fate at the end of the chase in front of an electric train. Afterwards, Carter had overheard a fake conversation and had passed it on to Adolf Karen.

He was scared, but he had more pluck than Hermann.

He watched Burke close the door of the room—a large kitchen, with a red fire glowing in the grate—and muttered:

'What's 'appened to 'Ermann?'

'He's had an accident,' said Burke. 'How many others here, Carter?'

'Three, mister,' Carter answered with alacrity.

'Where?'

'Hupstairs. Asleep, I reckon.'

'At half past nine?'

'They was out all night, mister—an' they bin busy all day. S'elp me ...'

'You aren't going to get any kind of help, unless you're very helpful yourself,' said Burke. 'Anyone due back who's not here?'

'Say, mister, that's arsking a lot ...'

'Someone might come, eh?'

'Yes.'

In Burke's experience, people who might come invariably did at the moment they were least wanted, and he knew that he hadn't long to act. He rather liked the frightened Cockney, a man who was scared but not craven, but it wasn't wise to judge from appearance, and Carter was in the way.

'I see,' said Burke. 'Open your mouth ...'

The man gaped, and Burke tucked a folded handkerchief into his mouth.

'Sit down,' he said.

Carter dropped into a chair, by the side of a deal table.

Burke had already noticed the folded tablecloth near the chair, and had decided what to do with it. He looped it round Carter's legs, to the chair, brought it up to the man's waist, thence to his wrists and the back of the chair. Carter looked uncomfortable, but there was a suggestion of relief in his eyes.

'You can move about on that chair,' said Burke, amiably, 'and you can make a lot of noise, if you try. I shouldn't try, if you like life.'

Carter gurgled something unintelligible.

Burke moved to the door, took the key from the inside,

went out and locked the door from the outside. The hall was in complete darkness, but Burke felt safe in switching on the light.

A narrow flight of stairs led to the upper quarters.

He mounted them, treading softly. No sound came until he reached the first landing, and then the harsh but rhythmic noise of snoring pierced the silence. He went softly onwards. The light from downstairs gave him sufficient illumination, and he could see four doors, one partly open. A little way ahead was a second flight of stairs.

He stepped towards the nearest closed door.

A faint sound from above made him stop. He stood poised, straining his ears to catch a repetition. It came—a light foot-fall, followed by a little cough.

Burke moved like lightning to the foot of the second flight of stairs, and his gun was in his hand. He had hardly reached the first stair when light flooded on from above him. He narrowed his eyes and tried to see. His gun pointed upwards.

He heard a slight gasp. He saw a pair of sensible brogue shoes and a pair of slim legs, a knitted skirt, and . . .

'You!' he said, and his whisper seemed to fill the silence.

Patricia Carris stared at him.

Patricia Carris!

Of course, it was absurd. She was in Scotland, with a benevolent-looking aunt and uncle.

It was the girl who spoke next, softly.

'What are you doing here?'

'That's one way of defence,' Burke said. 'Attack.' And then he stopped smiling and looked grimly at her. She was half a dozen stairs higher than he, but she regarded him steadily, and he examined every feature of a face that was already printed indelibly on his mind. Her eyes were very blue and direct.

He took another chance; he assumed that Patricia Carris had some explanation of her presence that would be reasonable and he trusted her.

'Let's not argue,' he said. 'Do you know the house well?'

'No—I've only been here a few hours.' She followed his example by keeping her voice very low.

'Anyone else up there?' he asked.

'I don't think so. There's my room, a bathroom, and another bedroom. There wasn't anyone in the bedroom ten minutes ago.'

'Are you game to help?' he asked.

'What is it?' She was smiling a little.

'Holding a gun,' he said, 'while I make some little men angry. There's a risk . . .'

'I'll chance it,' she said.

Burke didn't realise it, but the relief of seeing her, of feeling the friendly warmth of her smile, cheered him considerably. The distrust of Horace Miller had affected him more than he knew, and Patricia provided an anodyne for his annoyance.

'Let's get to it,' he said. 'Step very quietly.'

She joined him silently, and they went to the first of the unopened doors.

'I'll go in first,' Burke muttered. 'You'll follow me, and take the gun when I'm ready. Don't come in until I call.'

'All right.' She appeared to trust him completely.

Burke tried the handle. It turned easily, and he pushed open the door. The noise of snoring did not come from this room, and he strained his ears to catch any other sound. Soft breathing came . . .

He switched on the light and stepped in. Two single beds

were occupied by two men whom he had seen before, at Longtree House. One of them turned in his sleep, and Burke beckoned to Patricia.

'Keep close to the wall,' he said, 'and if I say so, shoot.'

Patricia nodded. Burke stepped to the nearest bed, reached his long arm over and caught at the edge of the top blanket.

His left arm tossed the rest of the clothes off, and before his victim had time to do anything more than grunt in alarm he was being rolled in the blanket, from head to foot.

Burke's eyes were hard as the second man woke up and reached for something under his pillow. Burke didn't hesitate. His fist crashed on to the man's jaw. His head went back and cracked against the wooden panel of the bed. He went limp.

'Fine,' muttered Burke.

Patricia's eyes widened a little, but the gun in her hand was steady. She watched Burke strip the sheet from the second bed, stuff the end of it in the man's mouth, and wind it round him, tightly. The second victim, rolled helplessly in the blanket, might have tried to move but for the sight of Patricia and her gun.

'A bit indelicate, I know,' said Burke, 'but it can't be helped.' He spent another sixty seconds in gagging the conscious man and making him more secure, then he sought for and found the guns beneath the pillows.

'That'll make us safer,' he said. 'But the next one isn't going to be so easy, Pat, unless our man with the snore is a very heavy sleeper.'

They went into the passage, listening intently. There was no sound now.

Burke's face was very grim.

'He's awake,' he muttered. 'Get to the head of the stairs, Pat, and keep your gun handy.'

She nodded, and walked softly to the head of the stairs. But there was fear in her heart as she saw him step to the second door, turn the handle and throw the door open. He leapt to one side.

Something sped past, thudding against the wall of the passage. Patricia saw Burke's hand move, and saw the flash of fire from his gun. A man's curse rang out, something hard and heavy clattered to the floor of the bedroom. Burke streaked into the room, and she heard the sound of scuffling. Every nerve in her ached to get to the room, but she waited.

Burke came out.

'One more door,' he said, 'and according to the latest stable talk, it's an empty room.'

'Be careful,' she whispered.

Burke nodded, and she saw the glint in his grey eyes, and lived through an age of agony as he repeated his manœuvre; but this time there was no sound after he had flung the door open.

'All we've got to do now, love, is make sure the top floor's empty.'

It was.

Less than half an hour after his arrival at the private hotel in Grand Drive, Wembley, Burke started down the stairs, with his hand on Patricia's shoulder, and with delight in his heart. He was not surprised that he had pulled it off; Hermann, Carter, and the three sleeping men were not, after all, very large obstacles. But it had been much easier than it might have been.

'Now,' he said, pressing her shoulder, 'we've got a few minutes to spare. I don't know where I shall be, later, so you might as well talk now.'

Patricia looked at him.

'You *are* sure of yourself,' she said.

'If I wasn't,' said Burke gently, 'I would have disappeared from this happy world years ago.'

Patricia looked at him, very steadily.

'You want to know why I'm here, of course?'

'Badly,' admitted Burke.

'I think that you'd perhaps understand better, if you read this,' Patricia said.

She handed a letter to him, and he took it, glancing quickly at the signature. His lips tightened.

'When did you have this?'

'Late last night.'

'In Scotland?'

'Yes.'

The letter was brief, and he could understand why it had brought her from Scotland. It ran:

My dear Pat,

You will readily understand that I don't like bringing this subject up again, but several little things concerning your brother's death have arisen, and I think you should know them. It isn't just that the manner of his death, supposed to be by misadventure, has a much more unpleasant side. I am seriously concerned, for fear you are unwittingly in danger, and I think it would be wise if you could come here for a day or two. I have not yet been to the police, and hesitate to do that until I've talked with you.

If I am not at the Club when you reach London, you will find me at the enclosed address. Please wire if you are coming and I will try to meet your train.

Yours,
Bart Hemming.

Burke read the letter twice and every word seemed to burn into his brain. His eyes were glittering as he looked at the cool, self-possessed figure of the girl.

'Was he at the station?'

'No. Nor the Club. So I came here.'

'What time did you get here?'

'About half past six,' said Patricia. 'I had a very bad journey, and I was glad to rest for an hour or two. I'd been resting when you came.'

Burke nodded.

'Who did you see, when you arrived?'

'A Miss Day, and the man, Carter.'

Burke frowned, a sudden vision of a fair-haired girl lying half-clad across the floor of a room where there was a dead man and a pool of blood, rose to his mind.

'Did you know Miss Day?'

'No. She introduced herself,' said Patricia. 'I think she is one of the owners of the place.'

'A fair-haired girl? Rather pretty?'

Patricia smiled a little.

'I think you could call her really pretty—Jim.'

Burke nodded.

'Good! Anyhow—you saw no one else?'

'No one.'

'You weren't disturbed at all?'

'I went up to the room half an hour after I arrived,' said Patricia, 'and I didn't wake up until I thought I heard someone moving on the landing. It was you.'

Burke pushed a hand through his hair.

'Well, we need to talk to your friend Bart Hemming. I wonder if Carter knows him. Let's go and see.' He led the way to the kitchen, where Carter sat exactly as Burke had left him, took out the gag and released the man.

'Sam,' he began.

And then he stopped, while Carter flinched and Patricia went pale. They were very silent as a thunderous banging on the front door was repeated.

17

ARREST OF AN AGENT

The smile that curved Burke's lips was one that Patricia Carris had learned to expect during her brief acquaintance with him, and somehow it spread to her. Only Carter still looked scared, and he had good reason to be. It was Carter who saw the face at the window.

'Cawww!' he gasped. 'Look...'

Burke looked, and Patricia, seeing the face, a lean one in which a pair of sharp eyes seemed to glitter, felt a tremor run through her. Burke continued to smile.

Carter made no effort to move, and Patricia, watching Burke move towards the front door, drew a deep breath and made for the back one and the face at the window. A well-dressed man stepped into the kitchen, his lean face twitching in the mildest of smiles. His low-pitched voice was cultured.

'Thanks,' he said. 'Don't move from here.'

As he spoke he went across the kitchen, covering the yards with remarkable speed. Patricia saw a gun in his hand, and she guessed that he had gone to follow Burke.

But Burke's voice came to her ears, a cheerful ringing voice that made her smile.

'Come in, boys,' he said, at the front door. 'You've come too late for the high spots, but there's a lot you can do yet.' His voice dropped, and he was no longer bantering as he said: ' 'Lo, Wally.'

'Hallo, Burke,' said Wally Davidson, a little less wearily than usual. In the bright light that flooded the passage, Burke could see the lean face of Agent 21 clearly, and Davidson looked like a man who was finding it difficult to do his job. He rubbed his cheek. 'I needn't tell you what I want, need I?'

Burke shook his head. He looked bleak, at that moment.

'No,' he said. 'But don't worry. I've done all I wanted, for the time being.' His expression brightened. He grinned. 'Spread over the house, lads,' he said to the half a dozen pleasant-looking young men who had flowed into the passage and were overflowing into the kitchen. 'There are three of 'em upstairs, one in the front room down, and a peaceful little man named Sam in the kitchen.'

These young men had learned not to take life seriously. All of them knew Burke slightly, and although they had orders to 'bring him in' they were prepared to treat him as one of themselves, providing he behaved. But they knew his quality, and three of them lounged in the kitchen, while he chatted with Patricia, and the others searched the house.

A solemn-faced man known as Righteous Dane, because his first name was St. John, entered the kitchen, while the heavy footsteps echoing up and down the house subsided. He cocked an eye and a thumb towards Wally Davidson.

'All correct,' he said. 'Four of them out there.'

'Alive?' asked Davidson, in the manner of a man always prepared for the worst.

'Yes,' said Righteous Dane, his tone reflecting his surprise.

'Which shows you,' said Burke, 'that I can be gentle, if I try.'

'Let's get,' said Dane.

Davidson nodded. Patricia felt a cheerful-looking youth touch her arm, and she walked with him towards the front door. She was frightened, by something she couldn't understand. Why had Burke stayed in the kitchen, as though under guard? Why was he followed closely by Davidson and Dane? She didn't know, and yet she felt there was good reason for alarm.

She saw Davidson touch Burke's shoulder, suddenly, saw Burke lift his arms, and Davidson run over him with his hands. Two revolvers and an automatic were transferred to Davidson's pockets.

Patricia seemed to feel a shadow about her.

There was an almost military precision about the operations of the raiding party. Three of their number were stationed in the house, two others stopped outside, and the rest bundled into two waiting cars, after seeing that Burke and Patricia were comfortably settled in. Carter was still in the kitchen under guard.

Burke was in a low-lying Delage tourer, while she was sitting next to Righteous Dane, who was at the wheel of an Austin. Dane smiled at her, and muttered:

'Sorry about this, Miss Carris.'

Patricia felt the car move from the kerb.

'But what is it?' she demanded. 'What has he done?'

Dane shrugged.

'No idea. He's wanted, that's all.'

Patricia said nothing for a moment, but her blue eyes were afire, and two spots of colour burned on her cheeks. The Austin followed the Delage into the main road before she said, very quietly:

'You're mad, all of you.'

'Why, yes,' said Righteous Dane, unabashed, 'but somebody has to be. Don't worry. Miss Carris?—*God!*'

The lean-faced driver of the Delage saw the thing coming at the same moment, and he literally trod on his brakes, wrenching the wheel round. Burke and Davidson, at the back of the car, were helpless. They felt the bump of the Austin behind them, a crash lessened by Dane's lightning grab at his brakes, but it was the thing ahead that fascinated them.

A lorry, backing from a side-turning, seemed to lose control and tear towards the Delage. As Burke watched, horror-struck, he saw the driver literally smashed to pieces. Something wet splashed into Burke's face, and he wiped it away, instinctively. And then he realised that the Delage had stopped, and he was still alive.

Gordon Craigie saw two things at the same time.

He saw a report of a wireless message that Bob Curtis, or Agent 17, had cut from the evening paper, and he saw the green light on the mantelpiece glow, just as it had glowed when Carris made his last, grim visit.

Craigie stood up, and pressed the control button of the sliding doors. He waited, guessing who was outside, and thinking of the wireless message. He could almost read it in the air. It ran:

Danish S.S. Vissen bound for Holland reports two Englishmen picked up in Baltic, both suffering exhaustion, critical condition. Vissen unloading at Amsterdam. Later: *Englishmen named Hopkins, travellers for Brown and Gardner, London.*

* * *

The Arrans had travelled under the name of Hopkins and as travellers from Brown and Gardner. The message explained the silence since they left for Rikka. Craigie had learned, from the Rikka contact, that Agent 31, Matthews, was dead. That was how Craigie had his news. Blunt messages, giving facts without trimmings. He walked into the passage outside his office, and saw the three men advancing towards him.

Righteous Dane was in front, with Davidson just behind, and Burke, towering above the others and with an arm round Davidson's shoulders. At another time it might have been absurd. Davidson had been sent to get Burke, and Burke was bringing him back; or helping him.

Dane was hard-faced.

'A smash,' he said, as he entered the office. 'Dyson's gone. A miracle we're here at all.'

The lines at Craigie's mouth grew deeper.

And then he looked at Burke, while the other two men seemed to fade. For a second that seemed an age Craigie and the big man regarded each other.

'Well?' said Burke.

Craigie's face was gaunt and grim.

'I've information from a reliable source,' he said, *'that you're working for Krotz.'*

Within an hour of the death of Nick Carris, four days before that meeting in Department Z, Craigie had sent messages to his European contacts, and the gist of the messages had been the same. Lathian Embassies were to be watched, and any recent activities reported.

The first of the reports had come when Burke was dodging death on the Kingston Road, and Craigie had done nothing but strengthen his watch on the big man. It had been to the effect that the Lathian attaché in Berlin had had, amongst other visitors, a certain Englishman, James Burke.

And then, just after Burke had been in the office, a second report had come from France, to the same effect. Before eight o'clock that night, Craigie was faced with the last thing he expected. Burke had been with the Lathian embassies of all the mid-European countries some time during the past two months.

Miller, meanwhile, had been making enquiries, and he discovered that Burke had been travelling Europe recently— for that matter, Burke had said as much—and Miller had been worried enough to report Burke's travels to Craigie. For the new agent had been to France since this affair had started. Then Miller had visited Bob Carruthers, and had found Carruthers staring ahead of him.

'What is it?' Miller had asked.

Carruthers, his head bandaged, and sitting in an easy chair at his flat, hadn't answered. Instead, he'd handed a sheet of paper on which were pasted several disjointed scraps of letters salvaged from the Cannon Street explosion. One sentence had stared up at the Superintendent:

If necessary get help from Burke.

Every possible argument had weighed with Craigie, even after that, to show Burke in a more favourable light, but the damning accumulation of circumstantial evidence had over-come those arguments.

Burke had followed the Arrans, and the manner of it had been dubious. Would any man have acted, on that first day, as he had, without some sound reason? And Burke had escaped from the Hurlingham house without harm. He had saved Carruthers, at Walham Green Station, but Carruthers had been his friend for many years, and after that incident *he had allowed Karen to escape.* He had justified himself to Craigie, who had wanted to believe Burke could see three moves ahead; but if Burke was working for Krotz, he was safe enough in setting himself up for a target, knowing Krotz's agents wouldn't harm him. True, there had been a smash outside Kingston, but Burke hadn't been hurt, and the affair might have been engineered, to create an impression. There was only Burke's word for the shooting in the Cannon Street office, and on his own admission Burke had omitted to search that place for papers—and not until the explosion had he thought to remedy it.

Craigie could not blind himself to the facts.

Later still, after Miller had telephoned from Hampstead, Craigie had been faced with Burke's assurance that he had found Smethwick dead. Wasn't it possible that Burke had killed Smethwick, using the American, Hemming, as a blind?

Finally Davidson had reported that Burke had disappeared from Hampstead, leaving the message about Wembley.

Craigie hadn't taken any chances after that. In fact, for the first time during the whole affair, Burke had escaped from his shadows on the run from Hampstead to Wembley, although in the first few days Craigie hadn't believed it necessary to question the big man's credentials. Craigie had taken ordinary precautions—and these were the results.

One of the most remarkable things about Craigie's London organisation was the speed with which he could get together a substantial party. With Davidson and Dane as joint C.O.s, the raiding party of Department men had gone to Wembley.

Craigie had doubted whether Burke would be there. It relieved him slightly, to see the big man entering the office. But it didn't affect the deadliness of his voice when he said:

'I've information, Burke, from a reliable source, *that you're working for Krotz.'*

18

BURKE TALKS

Burke drew a deep breath. His massive body moved a little, beneath the strain of that moment, for he knew that he was faced with damning evidence, or Craigie would never have made the statement. Worse, he couldn't prove to the contrary. In fact there was only one thing to do.

He said:

'Yes, Craigie, I am.'

Davidson, nursing a lacerated knee, gritted his teeth as the admission came. Righteous Dane's eyes were stony. Craigie stood, looking at the big man, without moving. For once in his life he had taken a gamble with his agents—and he had failed.

'I see,' he said.

Burke shrugged. His eyes, for the first time, lost their grimness, and the slightest gleam of humour shone in them.

'So is a man named Matthews,' he said.

Something clicked in Craigie's mind.

Matthews! The agent who had been working at the Villa Krotz for years, watching the revolutionary and sending rare but valuable reports to England. What did Burke know of him? Only two men knew, Craigie believed—or at least, two men had known; Carris and himself.

'Can I talk?' asked Burke.

Craigie nodded. He reached for his meerschaum, and for the first time lost that rigidity of bearing. He looked at Davidson, whose right trouser had been cut away, and whose lacerated knee showed through.

'Better get a doctor,' he said. 'Help Wally out, Dane, and come back when he's comfortable.'

Dane looked doubtfully at Burke, but he didn't argue.

He helped the limping man out of the office, and Craigie pressed the control button, to send the sliding door into position; then he dropped into a chair and motioned Burke to the other one. He didn't say so, but the second armchair was served with sufficient electric current to electrocute its occupant; Craigie had never taken chances.

Burke sat down.

'What do you know about Matthews?' asked Craigie, in his dry voice.

Burke took cigarettes from his pocket.

'Not very much,' he said. 'Only that Carris told me if I was ever stuck, at the Villa Krotz, I'd get help from Matthews.'

'Carris told you?'

'Yes.' Burke lit his cigarette. 'I met Carris nine months ago, just before the vitriol business. I was in Rikka to see the sights, and I'd met Carris at the Dalinka. He told me, too, that the Dalinka was a meeting place for Lathian contacts of the Department.'

Craigie nodded. Burke went on:

'Of course, Carris was sworn to secrecy, and you're probably thinking it's not true. But remember this. Carris was in danger, and he was being watched by Krotz. He knew that if he made a slip anywhere, it would mean Siberia. He went there. Did you know?'

Craigie nodded. His expression gave no indication of his thoughts.

'And then,' said Burke, '*Carris asked me to give him away, to Krotz.* He knew Krotz was working at some game, but his own chances of learning anything about it were small. Krotz was watching him too closely. And Carris argued that if I told Krotz that he, Carris, had asked me for help, as a spy, it would work me in with Krotz. Of course, I had to do it for money. Krotz had to be convinced that I was badly off. That,' went on Burke, 'wasn't difficult, because I suffered badly in one or two markets, a year ago.'

Craigie began to stuff his pipe. He said:

'That's why you've a furnished flat, is it, and you don't run a car?'

'That's why,' agreed Burke.

Craigie struck a match. He seemed to relax as Burke went on:

'Well, it worked. I sold Carris to Krotz. It wasn't until afterwards I learned of the vitriol business, and I think it would have been all up if I'd known of it at the time. Anyhow, Krotz started to use me. Remember, he was anxious to avoid all suspicion, and it was safer to send an Englishman to his various embassies, with messages, rather than contact through the usual channels. Of course, for the first month or two I was more or less on trust. But after a while I was sent on visits to the factory outside Rikka.'

'Smethwick and Karen?'

'It isn't known as Smethwick and Karen, over there. It's a privately owned mining and smelting factory, and a lot of other things.'

'Armaments,' said Craigie, very softly.

'Armaments,' said Burke. 'Fighter aircraft and small guns, mostly. The factory grounds cover twenty square miles, and it's almost impossible to get into it. I was only there for a few minutes, apart from the time I was in the smelting works, under guard. I was watched very closely, of course. Beyond discovering the real nature of the factories, I found out little, but that was enough to let me know Carris had been right. Krotz isn't manufacturing arms on a grand scale for nothing.'

'No,' said Craigie.

'My big trouble was,' said Burke, 'that I couldn't decode all the messages I took from place to place. I still can't decode them.'

'You still get them?'

'I haven't had one for four days,' said Burke. 'I had to deliver a message to the Paris Embassy.'

'Did you?'

'Yes,' said Burke. 'I went over by night plane, the day before yesterday, and I was back next morning. Did you know that?'

'Miller told me,' said Craigie. 'It was the first thing that made us really suspicious. But carry on.'

'I could have brought the message to you, and let the Government cypher folk have a shot at it,' said Burke, 'but it would have ruined all I'd been working for. Krotz worked like this. He told his Embassies a message was coming by me. The message was due at a certain time, and if it had been late Krotz would have been informed. You see, everything I did was closely checked. I think the messages I took to various embassies were fakes, intended to try me out all the time. Any interference with a message would have told Krotz I was playing him at his own game. So I didn't interfere with them.'

'Hmm,' said Craigie.

'Next,' said Burke, 'Krotz gave me instructions to come to England and wait for orders. I didn't get any for three days,

and then I heard the Arrans talking about the death of Carris
—or, more accurately, they told me they'd got the job of telling
his sister of his death. I followed them, and you know as well
as I do what has happened since.'

There was a brief silence. Then Craigie said: 'But as soon
as you started working against Karen, Krotz would learn of it.
Karen would contact him, wouldn't he?'

A grim smile played at Burke's lips.

'Yes, but I got my blow in first. I told Krotz by cable that I'd
managed to get in with you. I suggested to Krotz that he let
Karen carry on, thinking I was against him, you see,' he
diverged, 'I *had* to convince Krotz I was genuinely for him,
and if I was contacting with Karen, over here, while working
for you, Krotz would immediately jump to the assumption
that I was being checked all the time. In short, to work for you
and Karen was asking for trouble, and Krotz would realise it.
So I told him I'd take my chance of getting away from
anything Karen could fix for me. And I managed it.'

'But why didn't you tell me?' Craigie asked slowly.

Burke looked grim.

'As soon as I'd pitched my tale you would have asked your
people in Rikka for confirmation. Krotz might have discovered it. That would have meant the end of my service with
Krotz.'

Craigie looked at the lean, grim face of the man in front of
him, and pondered the various things he had told. From the
first, he had believed Jim Burke capable of thinking further
ahead than any man he knew. If this story was true, Burke had
been playing the most dangerous game conceivable, risking
trouble from Department Z as well as from Krotz, facing the
hazard of the Karen agency and thinking, all the time, not
three, but half a dozen moves ahead.

And Craigie believed the story.

He said:

'So all the time you've been working for me, but not doing enough damage to make Krotz suspicious; do you know the other agent?'

'No,' said Burke, 'but he's on Krotz's records as Number 3. And he's an Englishman.'

'You've always given him time to make good any damage *you* might have done to Karen. That's right?'

'Yes.'

'But how do you explain Karen's murder? There was a man in the Cannon Street office, listening to you all the time. You told me you'd tried to bribe Karen to talk.'

'If Karen had talked,' said Burke simply, 'I'd have done two things. Reported it to Krotz, and sent the result of the information to you. Karen would have been blamed, by Krotz, for giving you the information. I'd still be working for Krotz.'

'I've never heard anything like this, Burke,' Craigie admitted with real feeling. 'You're simply sitting with your face in front of a gun, and another one at the back of your head. You can't keep Krotz guessing any longer.'

'He's not guessing,' Burke said, 'he's *sure*. My talk with Karen will be reported, but Krotz gave me instructions to try Karen out; he had never been trusted. I've a solid and reasonable explanation that Krotz will take, to cover everything I've done in England, even down to the Wembley affair. Because the Wembley crowd were Karen's men. If Karen was likely to rat, so was his gang. It was best they were rounded up, from Krotz's point of view. Damn it, man, you can see that, can't you?'

Craigie nodded.

'And now,' said Burke, 'the English stunt is in the hands of Krotz's Number 3. The Department has only got him to tackle now, and with Karen's crowd safe, Number 3's got to do all his own dirty work. Unless'—Burke's eyes glinted—'Krotz tells me to help him.'

Craigie went motionless.

'And if he does,' said Burke quietly, 'we've got him where we want him: Krotz is smashed in England. And if Number 3 is as important in Krotz's international organisation as I think he is, we'll learn all we want to know about the game. If we know that, we can smash it.'

He paused. Craigie said nothing.

'Can't we?' persisted Burke.

Craigie drew a deep breath.

'Yes,' he said. 'You can have a free hand, Burke.'

There was a silence, while the two men regarded each other, the one with real gratitude, the other in an admiration deeper than he had ever felt before. Then:

'So that's that,' said Gordon Craigie. 'Now—do you think this man Hemming is Krotz's Number 3?'

'No,' said Burke. 'But I'll tell you what I do think.'

As if to make sure of absolute secrecy, he leaned forward, and his voice was very low.

There were several small, and mostly negative, developments in the next few hours.

First, Superintendent Horace Miller was told that Burke was all right, but that the detective's manner should remain hostile, for the time being. This was Burke's suggestion. Burke worked on the assumption that Number 3 was watching.

Second, they learned that the girl who had been found at Hampstead claimed to be a relative of Smethwick's, and maintained to the police that she knew nothing of the conspiracy. Burke knew, of course, that she was Miss Muriel Day, and that she had been living at the private hotel in Wembley. What connection she had with the Krotz business he did not know. He theorised that she had known of the plot to bring Patricia Carris from Scotland, knew she was at Wembley and believed she was in danger. She had learned, also, of Burke's unofficial connection with the affair, and had sent him to Wembley to look after Patricia.

What connection there was between Patricia and the affair Burke couldn't fathom. He would only be able to learn that from Hemming.

Hemming.

The genial Curtis, who had gone from the Hampstead house to the American Club, hoped to get there before Hemming, and failed. Hemming hadn't turned up. The police were watching for him, but there was no trace of that grey-haired, easy-mannered American.

The reason for the murder of Nathaniel Smethwick was still obscure. It was a reasonable assumption that Hemming had killed him. They learned a great deal about Smethwick, however, from the woman who had been arrested at the Hampstead house.

Her name was Marriott and she had served a term of imprisonment for theft. How she had obtained her situation with Smethwick was not known, but under cross-examination she admitted she had been robbing Smethwick systematically for some time. Smethwick was slightly unbalanced. So much was confirmed by the woman Marriott, and Colonel Bilton, who was telephoned by the police and asked to visit the Hampstead house on the purely formal business of identification.

Bilton had been troublesome. Weren't there plenty of people to identify the murdered man, without worrying a gentleman of his position?

All the Cannon Street office staff were dead, and the clerk was missing still. It was Colonel Bilton or the Hon. Marcus Cassey, decided Miller, and as Cassey was in Scotland, Bilton had to come.

Jim Burke was at the Hampstead house when Miller called Bilton on the telephone. He offered to fetch the obstinate Colonel.

'All right,' grunted Miller.

As it happened, Burke didn't see the car that passed along the road in which Bilton lived. He had little trouble with the Colonel, who had resigned himself to his grim job, and the two men were walking towards the taxi Burke had come in, when the car, without lights and moving very silently, passed them.

Just one stab of flame through darkness told Burke what had happened.

And Colonel Bilton threw up his arms, gurgled deep in his throat and went down. The bullet had smashed through his brain.

By night, telephone calls from England to the continent are speedy things. It was half an hour after the death of Bilton that a telephone rang in the Villa Krotz. Krotz himself lifted the receiver. The gruff voice of an Englishman came to his ears.

'Number 3, Herra Krotz.'

'Yes,' said Krotz.

'Bilton has gone,' said Number 3. 'Burke was with him.'

'Yes.'

'I haven't seen Hemming since he was at Smethwick's house. I told you the last time I telephoned.'

'Yes.'

'Karen's place at Wembley has been closed by the police. The girl Day has been taken, too, but she doesn't know enough to be dangerous.'

'No,' said Krotz. 'Who handled the Wembley raid?'

'Burke.'

'Burke,' said Krotz, 'is doing very well. You are sure that Karen was agreeing to a bribe, Number 3?'

'The information is reliable,' said Number 3. 'It came from Bray, who shot Karen and afterwards destroyed the office.'

'I thought that Rogers destroyed the office, and was afterwards badly injured.'

'Yes,' came the gruff voice of Number 3. 'That is true, but Bray arranged the bomb.'

'I see,' said Krotz.

'Any further orders?' asked Number 3.

'Yes. But let me think, Number 3. You have Lister and Bray left, with yourself and possibly Hemming.'

'If Hemming reappears, yes.'

'Of course. Are there any more?'

'No,' said the man with the gruff voice. 'But it's all finished now, isn't it?'

'Not quite,' said Krotz, very softly. 'There is Cassey, in Scotland, isn't he?'

'Yes.'

'Cassey must go, before he reaches London,' said Krotz. 'See to that, Number 3. Contact Burke, and tell him I must know immediately he learns if any message has been received in London from the Arrans.'

'You heard that two men were picked up by the S.S. *Vissen*,' said Number 3 quickly.

'Yes. I am sending to the ship, but the Arrans may not be so ill as they make out. I expect no trouble, and even if the papers from the Arrans should reach London, it will be twenty-four hours before they are decoded and translated. So we will have twenty-four hours in which to act.'

'Yes,' said the man in England.

'At the first word from Burke that a message has come from the Arrans,' said Krotz, 'you will act. The very first word, you understand. Everything else is prepared. That is all, Number 3.'

The man in England grunted, and the wires went dead.

19

BEFORE THE STORM

T he peoples of the East were taking their pleasures in the
West.

Ships were moving, ships of a great Eastern nation, filled
with men and women and children—but mostly with men.
There was nothing suspicious about these movements, for the
barriers of distance have been broken down, gradually, until a
Chinaman in London or a Japanese in Berlin is not remarkable. Some things that are remarkable, the number of Oriental
barbers along the Suez Canal, for instance, have also been
noticed by the shrewd and scoffed at by the clever. Why not?
The gradual penetration of the West by the people of the East
is not always so obvious, and when it is obvious, it is scoffed
at; and the shrewd ones are called scaremongers.

There were perhaps ten thousand men, Orientals, in ships
moving along the Suez Canal on pleasure, at the time of the
talk between Marius Krotz and his agent in England, Number
3. There was a fair sprinkling of Europeans, too, who enjoyed
the unfailing good humour of their Eastern brothers. At the
same time, five modern liners, three of them Oriental-owned

and two chartered to Oriental companies by American shipping lines, were in the Atlantic, on world cruises. At the same time, several English and American liners were cruising near China and Japan, and the one thing was no more remarkable than the other.

Three pleasure cruisers were in the Mediterranean, from the East, also, and one was as far north as the Gulf of Norway.

These things were known and even the shrewd were not suspicious. Why should they be?

They were dubious of the recent Manchurian activities, but it had long since been decided by European powers that the business of Manchuria was certainly not theirs, and if troops were massed on the northern borders of the puppet state, did it matter? It might have mattered if it had been known that a certain agreement had been reached by two major Eastern powers, but that piece of information was denied them. It had been made with such care that even Craigie had learned nothing of it. It wasn't even known that the massed troops had spread from Manchuria to Mongolia, keeping close to the northern borders, and at times entering the Soviet lands, while the north-western boundary of Sinkiang, part of the Chinese Republic, was generously peopled with soldiers.

Perhaps these things would have been obvious if there had been a mass movement of big guns and aircraft, but there was not.

Another thing that Craigie did not know was that a certain agreement had been reached, by the efforts of the Peking gentleman, by which the great Trans-Soviet railway, from Vladivostock to Leningrad, would cease to carry Russian passengers for a short period, to be decided at a future date, according to emergency. Even if the stopping of civilian traffic had been known, it would have been viewed as an eccentricity

of the most eccentric government in the world; the whims of
the Soviet covered a multitude of sins, just as the Trans-Soviet
railway could carry a multitude of people from the East to the
West with surprising speed—much greater speed than the
usual Russian railway service effected.

All these things were.

And other things would be, at a certain time. That time
depended entirely on two gentlemen of moderate stature,
twins, the one ugly and the other handsome, and both of them
lying in a berth on the S.S. *Vissen,* very close to death. In short,
the Arrans.

A man who might have been fifty, or might have been sixty-
five, walked along Brook Street towards Burke's furnished
flat. He noticed one or two men in plain clothes, near the flat,
and his lips curled a little. He was clean-shaven, and walked
with long, easy strides, which suggested he belonged to the
professional classes. He knocked at Burke's door, and was
admitted as far as the door of Burke's front room.

A girl opened the door, and the old man smiled, charm-
ingly, revealing immaculate dentures and speaking in a gruff
but cultured voice.

'Mr. James Burke?' he asked.

Patricia Carris, who had been worried all night by the
possibility that Burke was in danger, and had called at the flat
as soon as she had finished a hurried breakfast, said that Mr.
Burke wasn't in, but that he would be back any time.

'Is it urgent?' she asked.

'No,' he said, taking a small book and a number of leaflets
from his pocket. 'It's a little matter he was thinking of taking

up, Madam—insurance. I'll leave these with you, and in due course I expect he will write to me. Thank you.'

Patricia accepted the book and papers, but was absurdly disappointed, for she had expected something less ordinary than insurance, at that moment. Then she remembered some of the things that had happened, and smiled a little grimly at the possibility of Jim Burke taking out a life insurance policy.

The man raised his hat and went back to the street. He had hardly started to move towards Piccadilly before a burly man approached him. The burly man was polite, but:

'Sorry to worry you,' he said, 'but we're watching that house, sir.' He showed a police identity card. 'Who did you call on?'

The man looked taken aback, but he answered without hesitation.

'Mr. Burke—a Mr. James Burke. On a matter of insurance, sir.'

He fumbled in his pockets and brought out a sheaf of papers concerning the Enterprise Assurance Company, and after further fiddling produced a letter, dated nearly a year before. It was signed by Burke, and it asked the local agent of the Enterprise Company to call on him, periodically.

'You've called here before?' asked the detective.

'Why, yes, several times.'

'You know Mr. Burke?'

'No,' said the insurance agent, sadly. 'Mr. Burke travels a great deal. My predecessor saw him, I believe.'

He paused. The detective found that the papers, the collection book, several policies and letters, all bore out the fact that the clean-shaven man was a Percival G. Sutton, of the Enterprise Company.

'That's all right,' he said.

'I suppose,' said Mr. Sutton, tentatively, 'you're not interested in . . .'

'No thanks,' said the detective, politely.

He watched the man walk away, and told himself that Mr. Percival Sutton knew all there was to know about enterprise. Then he saw the massive figure of Jim Burke entering Brook Street, and pondered on the activities of the big man.

Burke nodded at the watching detectives and entered the flat. He knew Patricia was there, for he had been in when she had called; he had suggested that she would probably be safer at Brook Street than anywhere else.

'Karen pinched you, early on,' he had said, with a smile, 'and you nearly walked into Hemming's open arms. In fact, you've been very nearly kidnapped twice, and the third time might be fatal. There's a lot of men about here, and you'll be as safe as houses. Will you stay?'

Patricia had stayed.

Burke smiled at her as he entered the room, and he stood still for a moment, looking at her. She was very lovely, and he had fallen deeply in love. He stepped towards her, and before she realised what he was doing, kissed her.

He drew back.

'That's more than Hemming ever did,' said Patricia, a little maliciously, but the colour in her cheeks became her.

'That's right,' said Burke, 'be nasty. Anyone called?'

'An insurance man,' said Patricia, 'A nice old man, Jim.'

Burke rubbed the side of his nose.

'Did he leave anything?'

'Yes—a sheaf of papers and a book.'

Burke took them from her and glanced down.

He kept looking for several minutes, and then he lifted his face, and she saw the gaunt, grim lines that had been there on the previous night. He laughed, but without humour.

'An insurance agent, eh?'

Patricia's hand touched his arm.

'Jim. It's not trouble?'

Burke seemed to shake himself, and when he was finished he was smiling, and stuffing the papers in his pocket.

'The Lord knows, sweetheart,' he said lightly. 'It's interesting, but not for you to worry your head about.'

'Can I help it?' asked Patricia very softly.

Burke looked at her.

'One day, Pat, God willing, we'll be on top of the world. But at the moment it's a pretty ugly place, too mucky for you to think about. Pat, promise me to stay here during the next few days, and not go out on any pretext?'

Patricia's blue eyes were very sad.

'You think that's necessary, Jim?'

'Sure of it,' said Burke.

She nodded, and Burke pressed her arm.

'Things to do,' he said, 'and not much time to do them in. By the way—you remember Carter?'

Patricia laughed as she remembered the morose Cockney at Wembley.

'Yes.'

'He's in this affair by accident,' said Burke. 'He's a gentleman of the criminal fraternity who'll mend his ways if he's properly encouraged. I've fixed up with Miller not to charge him, and he'll be round here, some time today. He won't leave the flat, and there'll be a policeman here, too, just in case we've underestimated him. But treat him gently, because there might be a day when I'll want a maid-of-all-work.'

Burke smiled, and waved—and the door closed behind him. Patricia went to the window and watched him swinging towards Piccadilly. She felt sad, and there was real anxiety in her heart.

As Burke passed the plain-clothes men in Brook Street, he lifted his left hand towards them, and they understood from that that he didn't want to be followed. Walking easily, he went towards Piccadily, crossed to Haymarket, and eventually entered the offices of the Enterprise Assurance Company.

The offices were not large nor luxurious, but they covered three floors of the building, and there was an air of respectability about them. Burke wasn't concerned by the respectability. He was thinking of the papers he had received.

In them was a note from Percival Sutton, who signed his name with a flourish. At the end of the N was a very definite 'K'. Burke had been prepared for that K, and he needed no telling that Krotz's Number 3 was an official of the Enterprise Company.

A pale-faced clerk took his card.

'Mr. Sutton,' said Burke.

'Yes, sir. This way, sir.'

Just two minutes later, Jim Burke was shaking hands with the clean-shaven gentleman who might have been fifty, or even sixty-five. Sutton was a tall man, well-built, reminding Burke of a certain Mr. Cuthbertson—or Karen.

But Karen was dead.

The two men eyed each other without speaking, sizing each other up. It was Sutton who broke the silence.

'I can't imagine why you work for the Lathian gentleman, Burke,' he said, in a slow, gruff voice.

A wisp of a smile was on Burke's lips.

'Why do you?' he asked.

Sutton shrugged his big shoulders.

'Money, of course.'

'Money, of course,' said Burke. 'You were asking for trouble, going to Brook Street.'

Sutton nodded.

'I only just evaded it,' he admitted. 'But I had to contact you, and I didn't want to telephone. Telephones,' he added, with a sudden smile, 'aren't as reliable as they might be. They leak.' His manner changed. 'I spoke to K, last night.'

'Yes,' said Burke.

'He's still convinced that you're a reliable agent,' said Mr. Sutton, more gruffly than usual. 'I hope you are.'

'I hope that you're not trying to teach K his business,' said Burke genially, 'Number 3.'

There was silence.

Burke felt the keen, light-grey eyes of the other man boring through him, but he faced the scrutiny without a qualm. Often he had felt the black eyes of Krotz on him, and he had stood it; Sutton was nothing, compared with Krotz.

Sutton said at last:

'No, I'm not trying to teach K his business. I'm just warning you. You don't need telling we are very near the climax, do you?'

'No,' said Burke.

'We might have to move quickly, if the Arrans get a message to Craigie,' said Sutton. 'Can you find that out?'

Burke felt very cold inside. So the Arrans had been successful in their mission, before they had been wrecked.

'Yes,' he said. 'I'll ask Craigie soon.'

'Ask him regularly,' said Sutton, 'and telephone here. Ask for me, and say "yes" or "no". I won't want anything else.'

'Supposing you're not here?' asked Burke.

'I'll be here, that message will be important,' said Sutton. 'It's lucky my men shoot straight, isn't it?' he asked.

A cold fury surged through Jim Burke.

'You mean—Bilton?' he said.

'Bilton and Karen,' said Sutton. 'You've been very useful, keeping Craigie's men after Karen while I've been working.'

'Good,' said Burke, and his teeth were clenched.

'You're not very curious,' said Sutton.

'I'm not paid to be curious,' said Burke with a ghost of a smile. 'Is there anything else?'

'No,' said Sutton. He seemed to want to talk. 'When I heard of this Karen business,' he said. 'I was inclined to think you were double-crossing us.'

'Krotz,' said Burke, with slight emphasis.

Sutton shrugged and laughed.

'All right, Krotz, then. We're all in the same family, after all. Feathering our nests with the jewels of the East.' He laughed again, but his eyes were narrow, and he was watching Burke closely.

Burke was thinking: 'The jewels of the East.'

He said, as ideas flashed past each other in his mind:

'They're all waiting, of course.'

Sutton's face lost its expression.

'So you know that, do you?'

'My dear man,' said Burke, with a short laugh, 'can you imagine Krotz trusting anyone unless he was absolutely sure it was safe?'

'No,' admitted Percival Sutton, very slowly. 'What are your plans when it's all over?'

Burke shrugged his shoulders.

'I haven't any. Don't you think it'll be healthy enough to stay over here?'

'It won't be healthy enough to stay anywhere in Europe,' said Sutton with a harsh chuckle. 'Our only bet will be the enemies of our friends in America.'

Burke nodded, as if he fully understood. He didn't, but his

mind was filled with questions and ideas. 'The enemies of our friends—in America.' He repeated the words, half a dozen times. Then he understood.

For the greatest enemy of America was the East.

'Yes,' he said, standing up.

He had all the information he needed, now. He was sure enough of his grounds to telephone for the police, or Craigie, and have Sutton taken away. The only thing that made him stop was the possibility that someone else, someone besides Sutton, was watching or listening to that conversation. If a message was flashed to Krotz that he had held Sutton up, the thing might still explode.

He had only the vaguest idea of what would explode, but he was beginning to comprehend the size of it. And it was madness to risk it just to take Sutton. Krotz was the man he wanted—Krotz.

'Yes,' he repeated, 'I suppose so. We'll see. Meanwhile I'll call you if Craigie's had any message from the Arrans.'

'That's right,' said Sutton.

He stopped suddenly, and his eyes narrowed. He seemed not to move, but an automatic glistened in his hand. A dreadful fear surged through Burke.

And then the grimness went out of Sutton's eyes.

'You shouldn't come in like that,' he said to someone behind Burke. 'You should knock, Hemming.'

Hemming!

Burke looked round. Hemming, suave and smiling as ever, nodded pleasantly. His hands were in his pockets and he looked the perfect example of the well-to-do American.

'Sorry,' he apologised, grinning at Burke. 'Well, my big friend—we've got you then?'

Burke said nothing. He was longing to get his hands round the throat of the American, for he remembered suddenly, vividly, the cut throat of Nathaniel Smethwick, and the letter to Patricia Carris.

Sutton laughed.

'That's all right, Hemming,' he said. 'Our friend Burke is one of us. He always has been.'

Hemming whistled. He had stopped smiling, and Burke wondered why. Sutton was frowning. He started to speak, but Hemming drew his hands from his pockets, and both hands held automatics.

'Fine,' he said softly. 'Then I've got two of you, together.'

The silence in the office was deadly. All three men were there, like statues, and the guns in Hemming's hands were very still. Burke was trying to think, but this had stopped him. He couldn't fathom it. Sutton had told Hemming that Burke was working with them—and Hemming had said:

Then I've got two of you, together.

It didn't make sense.

Sutton wasn't thinking at all. His eyes had narrowed to the merest slits. He said:

'So you're renegading, Hemming.'

Hemming laughed.

'That's a way to put it,' he said. 'You made one big mistake, my friend, when you tried to blame the murder on me last night. I'll stand for any kind of crooked stuff, excepting murder.'

Burke looked at Sutton.

Sutton swallowed hard. He licked his lips.

'Listen, Hemming.' His voice was high-pitched now, and without gruffness. 'This is a bigger thing than you realise. I hired you to watch the Carris girl for me.'

'Sure. And I watched her.'

'And you did it well,' said Sutton. 'I haven't a single complaint, you'll be well paid.'

'Not well enough to stand a charge of murder,' said Hemming grimly. 'You over-stepped yourself. I've been dodging the police all day, and I don't like it. You're going to tell them exactly what happened.'

Burke watched Sutton.

'Am I?' asked Sutton.

His hand moved, with the incredible speed Burke had seen before. But Burke had been watching for it. As the gun flashed in Sutton's hand, Burke jerked the desk in front of the man. The bullet hummed towards the ceiling, and a fraction of a second later a bullet from Hemming's gun bit into Sutton's throat.

'Well, well,' said Bart Hemming, 'I owe you plenty for that, Burke. But we're in trouble now. He's dead.' The American put his automatics back in his pocket, seeming to take Burke on trust. 'The murder last night was bad enough.'

Burke broke from the trance that had caught him.

'Don't worry about Sutton's death,' he said.

Hemming laughed nervously.

'Sutton?' he said. 'Sutton died last night. *That* man is Smethwick. Didn't you know?'

20

BLIZZARD

I took Burke several stunned minutes to accept the truth. The man whom he knew as Sutton was Smethwick. The man whom he had thought was Smethwick was Sutton, Personal Policy Manager of the Enterprise Assurance Company. And Smethwick, Managing Director of Smethwick and Karen, that reputedly unbalanced old man, was Krotz's Number 3!

He understood Bilton's death suddenly. Every possible step had to be taken to prevent identification of the man whose throat had been cut. Anyone who had known him well, Bilton for instance, had been killed. There was a likeness between the two men, but not a sufficient one to deceive people who knew them closely. The only problem that had faced Krotz's agents had been to prevent anyone finding out that the dead man was not Smethwick. Such a discovery would have meant a hue and cry at a time when Smethwick needed to concentrate on the Lathian adventure.

The woman Marriott had been bribed, of course. And she

was afraid to speak, lest the murder of Sutton should be blamed on her.

So Bilton's murder was fully explained, as well as the ruthless killing in Cannon Street. Officially, Smethwick was to die, to keep suspicion from him. It was clever and cunning.

Burke woke up suddenly.

'You're not in a fix,' he told Hemming. 'Stand by and don't worry. You can tell us your story later.'

He picked up the telephone and called Miller at the Yard, told that worthy what had happened, and finished:

'Send a warning up to the Hon. Marcus Cassey in Scotland,' he said. 'He'll be next for the high jump, I fancy. Smethwick will have sent someone after him, by now.'

'All right,' said Miller. 'Be careful, Burke.'

'Like hell I'll be careful!' said Burke.

His mind was working quickly now, and he took in the whole picture. He would have to move quicker than he had ever moved in his life before.

Hemming was frowning uncertainly. Burke snapped:

'Take the other telephone, will you, and call Piccadilly 57185. A man named Carruthers. Ask him if he's well enough to tackle an aeroplane, and then hold him on.' He picked up the first instrument again, and this time called Craigie.

The Chief's dry voice came over the wires.

'All hell's loose,' said Burke, without realising the grimness of his voice. 'Will you send several men over here, with some of your cypher experts?'

'Where?' asked Craigie. There was no suggestion of urgency in his voice.

'Enterprise Assurance,' said Burke.

'I'll come myself,' said Craigie.

Burke replaced the receiver, and wiped his forehead with

the back of his hand. He looked at Hemming who had the receiver to his ear.

'Well?' snapped Burke, reaching for the telephone.

'He says "yes".'

Burke nodded. Carruthers' voice came over the wires.

'What the hell, Jim . . .'

'Cut it,' interrupted Burke. 'Get to Heston and fuel your plane, Bob. It'll carry us to Lathia, won't it?'

'Have to refuel in Germany,' said Carruthers.

'That's all right. Have them prepare another plane, in case we need it, and do this faster than you've ever done anything in your life.'

He rang off. And then he smiled, for Hemming was unscrewing the top of a whisky flask.

'You'll be needing this,' said the American.

The drink gave him new energy, and he lit a cigarette thoughtfully. Then:

'Let's hear your part in this,' he said.

Hemming's story was simple.

Under his real name of Rannigan, which Burke heard for the first time, he had travelled from America to England on the same ship as the genuine Bartholomew Hemming. Between the two men there was a likeness, not deep, but sufficient to pass muster with casual acquaintances who had only seen the real Hemming occasionally and at long intervals. Moreover, Hemming had suffered a long illness and he had altered a great deal. After spending several months in the South of France for his health, Hemming had made a short business trip to New York, and it was after that that the two men met on the liner.

Always seeking an opportunity for making money, he had begun a friendship with Hemming. At Southampton, however, Hemming had decided to go on to France, and he had asked

Rannigan to advise the people at the American Club, who were expecting him, of his change of plans. Satisfied that Hemming was going to lose himself in Europe for some time to come, Rannigan had decided to impersonate him at the American Club, where the real Hemming's credit was high.

It had been easy. The servants believed his changed appearance was due to his long illness. Not until he had met Smethwick, who had known Hemming well, was his impersonation discovered.

Smethwick had promised to disclose nothing providing he kept a watch on Patricia Carris. Rannigan, as Hemming, had not hesitated to take his chance.

The first time he had known of a killing had been at Hampstead where, after writing the letter to Patricia, in Scotland, he had been summoned by a telephone call. It was obvious that Smethwick, having killed Sutton, wanted suspicion to fall on Hemming.

'And why did you have to watch Miss Carris?' Burke asked.

Hemming shrugged.

'I fancy she was brought down from Scotland to keep you busy. Smethwick didn't say so, but he hinted it.'

It was more than possible, of course. Smethwick wasn't sure of Burke; he had revealed that in the office. And he had tried to get Patricia in order to distract Burke from the main issues.

'And where does the girl Day come in?' asked Burke.

Hemming smoothed his greying hair.

'Muriel and I have worked together for a long time,' he said unblushingly. 'The old game, Burke, confidence tricks. That's how Smethwick got to know us. Muriel's been looking after the Wembley place, but Smethwick called her to Hampstead last night. We were to have been caught for the murder together.'

Burke nodded, and thought of Nathaniel Smethwick, whose dead body was in the chair behind him. There were few crimes Smethwick hadn't touched, but he didn't matter now.

Only Krotz did.

Craigie came almost as soon as Hemming had finished his story. The Chief, buttoned up against the cold March winds, saw, but didn't comment on, the body of Smethwick.

Burke talked in brief, vivid sentences.

'There's the whole thing,' he finished. 'Japan and China, the East, invading Europe. It's been prophesied for years. *And Krotz has been manufacturing arms, guns, aircraft, ready for them when they come! All they have to do is move their men.*'

Craigie didn't speak.

He had built the same mental picture, while Burke had been talking, and he had no doubt that it was true. He felt sick. For Burke had told him what Smethwick had said, 'they're all waiting'.

The East was ready.

Burke said:

'With any luck, there'll be enough information in this office to tell us where they are and how they're coming to Europe. Krotz will give the word, of course, and start it by some flare-up, in mid-Europe. But Krotz won't yet, if he can get hold of the documents the Arrans took from him. So we've a few hours left.'

'What are you thinking of doing?' asked Craigie.

'*I'm going to get Krotz,*' said Burke.

Two aeroplanes took off from Heston aerodrome within a few seconds of each other. Carruthers, his head still bandaged, but his eyes glowing, was piloting a two-seater Hawk, with Burke behind him. Righteous Dane was in the other plane, while Robert Curtis told himself he was going to get cold, before the journey was over.

The planes roared across space. The North Sea was beneath them, absurdly small from their ten-thousand-feet height. France and the Continent stretched ahead of them, and England behind them. Germany was in their path.

They stopped at the Hamburg Central Airport, and were given every help to speed them on their way. Craigie had been working.

They were fifty miles away, flying over the Baltic towards Lathia, when the first flakes of snow fell. Ahead of them, the leaden clouds gave promise of the blizzard to come. Soon they plunged into a whirling sea of moving white flakes, blinding them, freezing them. The sea and the sky were blotted out. Their arms and legs were stiff with cold, they could hardly move their hands. Carruthers, his lean face set with usual grimness, muttered into the speaking contact:

'We'll be lucky to make a landing, Jim.'

'We were born lucky,' said Burke.

The temperature dropped faster than ever. Only the pilots realised, to the full, the dangers of the next half hour—and both of them believed it was the end.

They could fight anything except the dreaded weight of the snow on the wings of the planes, on the bodies, on the fuselage. It was bearing them down—down.

Carruthers' eyes were on the altitude gauge. They were dropping with the weight of snow on them. The light two-seaters couldn't stand it.

Two thousand feet . . .

Fifteen hundred . . .

One thousand . . . downwards.

The seething, icy waters of the Baltic were below them,

hungry waters, invisible, but audible now. They pressed on through the blanket of freezing whiteness, all four of them realising the truth. *They couldn't last out!*

Burke no longer felt the cold.

He had not thought of failure. He had started out on his last mission, to get Marius Krotz. Now Number 3 was dead he doubted whether anyone would have sent a message to the man who had schemed this thing, the Western who had been bought by the Orient. He believed, once he reached Rikka, and the Villa Krotz, that he could get at the man. Krotz would have no warning.

Only by getting at him, now, could this thing be prevented. The invasion of Europe was inevitable, while Krotz lived. Directly that avarice-maddened revolutionary realised the English connection was broken, he would act. Unless he had a message from Smethwick soon, the damage would be done. There was a regular communication between Krotz and his Number 3, and a breakdown between them would be as effective as a direct warning.

And Smethwick was dead; he couldn't communicate with Krotz now. *Krotz would act!*

Burke seemed to see Europe, beneath him, ravaged by fire and death. And then he gave a wild, reckless laugh.

Europe was covered by snow. It wasn't red, it was white! And they were being forced downwards, to a freezing death. It was inescapable.

Carruthers kept grimly to his controls, but he had lost hope. The weight of snow was too much.

Dane, behind him, tried to find an extra ten miles of speed. For the first time for an hour the two planes were in sight of each other. Curtis was still grinning a set grin; Righteous Dane was swearing, aloud, obscenely.

The second plane was fifty feet below the first; and it ran

into a squall.

For a few minutes it had been flying directly below Burke, who was staring down at it, seeing yet unseeing. Not until the wings tilted did he realise what was happening. He bellowed to Carruthers. Carruthers looked down. He swore.

Dane's machine, seen vaguely through that universe of whirling flakes, twisted and turned like a mad thing, tossed helplessly by the wind. Burke could just see the faces of the two men. And then the plane dropped out of sight.

Four hundred feet below it smashed into the furious waters of the Baltic, and the sea closed over it.

Above, Carruthers battled grimly, knowing he was fighting a losing battle, but keeping on. He mustn't give in.

And then they broke through the blizzard, and the world ceased to move. Ahead of them they could see the white-clad city of Rikka, capital of Lathia, centre of the holocaust that threatened Europe and the world.

Burke set his stiff lips to the speaking tube.

'That single white building, Bob, dead north.'

Carruthers nodded.

They were flying over Rikka now, still less than a thousand feet up, but safe enough. The Villa Krotz, standing in its wide grounds beyond the city, had been fixed clearly in Burke's mind. No other building was within two miles of it, apart from the small huts on the estate, that were covered with snow and looked like part of the fields.

The plane roared on, over the city.

Carruthers cut off the engine, and they glided downwards towards the blanket of snow.

The wheels touched the ground. The plane went up a few

feet into the air, came down again, bumped—ran along the thick white carpet. Carruthers stopped it.

'Thank God!' Burke said. And then he saw that Carruthers had fallen stiffly across the controls.

Dimly he was conscious of voices, of black things moving across the whiteness, towards him. He leaned back against the plane, and he knew that for a while he was useless.

Time passed.

Strong hands lifted Carruthers from his seat, and hurried him towards the Villa Krotz. A huge, bear-like man, with small, cruel eyes, grabbed Burke's arm and forced him away from the machine. Burke's legs worked, stiffly, painfully. Gradually they grew looser. The pain eased.

'Better, Herra Burke?' growled Marx.

Burke nodded.

Marx ran him towards the Villa, knowing the danger that would result if he let the other get stiff again. The great hall of the Villa was open, and Burke went in. The heat seemed to whip his face. He gasped for breath.

'Drink, Herra Burke.'

Burke drank potent dry whisky, that seemed to burn his vitals, but it gave him strength. For the first time he was able to move unaided. Marx was grinning broadly. Carruthers was stretched out on a skin rug, unconscious.

'Where is Herra Krotz?' muttered Burke.

'Waiting,' said Marx.

'It is urgent,' said Burke. 'Urgent. Hurry.' Together they walked towards the stairs and to the red-doored room on the first landing. Marx knocked on the door; Burke stood by, waiting, wondering, his mind in torment. A high, thin voice called: 'Come in.'

Marx opened the door and Burke went in.

Marius Krotz rose from a high-backed chair and walked

towards him, his black eyes glowing, and the yellow rims to them deeper than usual. But he spoke gently.

'Well, Burke?'

Burke felt a mad whirling in his head. He swallowed hard.

'I had to come,' he said. 'By plane. Number 3 . . .'

'Yes?' Krotz took a step forward.

'Dead,' gasped Burke. 'Shot. Office occupied. You've got to move, Herra Krotz.'

There was a short, tense silence. And then:

'I thought there was trouble,' said Marius Krotz. 'You have done well, Burke. But I didn't wait for you. *It has started!*'

21

THUNDER IN EUROPE

I t had started.

Across the world a message had been flashed, from the West to the East and back again. It had started. The East was marching towards the West, or sailing or flying. There was thunder in Europe, that low, distant, rumbling thunder that heralds the biggest storms. Across Russia, train-loads of Orientals were rushing, all points worked by small, clever men, who used the trans-Russian railway more efficiently than it had ever been used before. Pleasure ships in the Mediterranean were making for Greece, the starting point for the great offensive from the south. Ships in the North Sea headed for the Baltic, ships in the Atlantic were turned towards France, and overnight those ships became grim carriers of death.

In Lathia, Frederik was shot by a Croat, and a thousand men, inflamed by the madness of Marius Krotz, brought Lathia to the peak of frenzy. Soldiers marched towards the frontiers, burning for vengeance. In three mid-European countries, kings and queens were butchered, and madness was let loose, while the men marched towards the frontiers.

The European hell was loose again, on that first day.

And on the second day.

A convoy of German planes flew towards France, carrying bombs and scattering death. A madman, shouting 'Vive la France', loosed a round of bullets at the leader, in Berlin.

Two Powers went mad.

War . . .

Great ships nearer the coasts of Europe, waiting for the flames to get firm hold inland, and the navies of the East were rushing across the world. Squadrons of battle-planes, were coming across the Arabian Sea, to spread destruction everywhere and anywhere in Europe.

In England a frenzied Government met and tried to stem the tide of battle, but the chance was slim, if it wasn't dead. America, unaware as yet of the Yellow Menace, did not believe the war could come, could not realise the power magazine had exploded.

France wanted war, Germany wanted war. They had been straining at the leash for years. The frontier firing in smaller countries had already started.

The thunder was rumbling across Europe.

'But—I didn't wait for you,' said Marius Krotz. '*It has started!*'

Burke stared at him.

He couldn't think. He was stunned.

Krotz smiled thinly.

'You're over-wrought, Burke. A remarkable achievement to fly from England since this morning. Marx, look after Herra Burke.'

Burke shook his head, like a bull.

'I want a drink,' he said.

'Come,' said Marx, spreading his great paws about the Englishman's elbow. 'We will get it.'

Burke looked at him. Marx saw eyes that were as hard as diamonds, and he showed his foul teeth.

'Come, Herra Burke.'

'*God!*' said Burke.

He lifted his hands swiftly, clenched them, and his right fist went like a steam-hammer towards Marx's grinning mouth. Marx took the full blow and hurtled backwards. His head struck against an iron box.

'*Burke!*' Krotz moved his right hand towards his pocket. The knife that had slit Matthews' throat flashed.

'Krotz,' said Burke, and his fist went against the Lathian's mouth, driving Krotz backwards with his feet lifted from the ground. The knife flew upwards, then hit the wall. Krotz pawed the floor with his hands and feet.

Burke saw nothing but a red mist and the face of Marius Krotz. He went forward and his left hand found Krotz's throat.

'Remember Carris, Krotz? And Matthews? And two girls in England?'

He stopped talking and yanked Krotz to his feet. In his last moment on earth the Lathian tried to speak, but Burke saw just his face, through the red mist, and he struck. He hardly felt his fist on Krotz's jaw, and he didn't hear the snap of the Lathian's neck. Krotz went down, like a log. Burke wiped his hand across his eyes and the red mist cleared away.

'Well,' he said absurdly, 'that's that little job done.'

He looked at the unconscious body of Krotz's servant, and then kicked the door to. Krotz had felt safe with Marx, and there were no other servants near. Burke ran his hands over the big man's clothes and found what he wanted. Keys.

The idea had been ticking through his brain for a long time, even in the aeroplane, and now he knew it was the only one left that might help.

He couldn't bring himself now to kill Marx, but gagged the man and bound him hand and foot, tying him finally across Krotz's bed. Then he went down the great staircase into the hall that was half-filled with waiting men. Carruthers was sitting in a chair, conscious again. He saw Burke and his eyes gleamed.

'We're too late,' said Burke, in English. 'But we've got one chance. If you call it a chance.'

'Let's have it,' said Carruthers.

Burke told him. Carruthers nodded and there was a smile on his lips, despite the fact that Burke had told him he was, in all probability, going to his death.

'Are you fit enough?' Burke asked.

'For that,' said Carruthers.

Burke nodded and looked around the hall. He knew several of the waiting men and they smiled at him, friendly enough. He had been known for a long time as the big English friend of the great Herra Krotz.

And then the second idea came to Burke.

He snapped in Lathian:

'Herra Krotz wishes an aeroplane. The Air Commandant is here, yes?'

A tall, thin man, with a slit of a mouth and cunning, close-set eyes, came forward.

'It is I, Herra Burke.'

'We will go at once,' said Burke. 'Where is the nearest machine from here?'

'There is one in the Villa hangar, Herra Burke.'

'Loaded? Like those for . . .'

He didn't finish the sentence, although he guessed that planes had left Lathia on a grim message. The man's eyes glittered.

'For Paris, Herra Burke. Yes?'

'Let us go at once,' said Burke.

His hand was in his pocket, all the time, about the butt of his gun. A single false step might mean discovery. The three of them went through the great house, and out into the snow-bound fields. At the rear of the Villa Krotz was a hangar, holding two fighter-bombers. A two hundred yard stretch had been cleared of snow, ready for a take-off, and men were still working at it.

'We are taking Herra Krotz?' asked the Air Commandant.

'No,' said Burke.

The man hesitated.

'You have his written order, Herra Burke?'

'Yes,' snapped Burke. 'I've got it. Hurry, man.'

It worked. Burke was too friendly with Herra Krotz for the other to risk any trouble. Three of them clambered into the machine. It worked by automatic starting. Burke entered last, and the machine began to move.

'Can you handle it when we get up?' Burke asked Carruthers, in English.

'I can have a damned good try,' said Carruthers.

Burke grunted, and sat next to the pilot. It was a large machine capable of carrying five men, as well as a load of bombs. Two machine-guns were in the cabin where they sat.

The machine climbed towards the clouds.

'Warmer than your other one, Herra Burke?' The Air Commandant laughed, complacently.

'And more useful,' said Burke, forcing a smile. 'They are the bomb releases?' He touched levers just beneath the pilot's hands.

'Yes! Have care.'

'Sorry,' grunted Burke.

The great machine went up steadily: One thousand, fifteen hundred, two thousand, two-five-hundred. The leaden clouds seemed less threatening now. Three thousand feet.

'Safe enough now,' said Carruthers.

'Good,' said Burke.

He turned in his seat, and the Air Commandant felt a great hand, with fingers that might have been made of steel, at his throat. He tried to struggle, but was held as in a vice. His hands dragged away from the controls. The machine began to tilt sideways.

Burke hauled his man out of the seat, and Carruthers clambered into position. The machine was twisting and turning now. Carruthers looked at the controls.

'We're in a spin,' he said. 'Don't worry.'

Burke's stomach seemed to turn over. The machine was nosing downwards. The white blanket beneath seemed to move towards them. The machine shuddered, and then slid smoothly along. The rocking stopped.

Carruthers grinned.

'You can't miss our spot,' said Burke. 'Keep due north for a mile or two—if it wasn't for this blasted snow we'd have seen it by now. Ah . . .'

He turned quickly as the Air Commandant wriggled; then he doubled his fist and rapped the man beneath the jaw, three times in quick succession.

Burke climbed into the seat next to Carruthers. He saw the vague white shapes of the great munitions factory that Krotz had been building for years. In less than two minutes they were flying over it, and then Burke said:

'Here we go, Bob!'

He touched the first bomb release. The second, the third.

They saw the things falling beneath them, long, dark blobs against the virgin snow. The first one hit the ground and it seemed that nothing happened for a long time. And then a mass of dark earth and smoke spread outwards, as if it was curving slowly away from the spot where the bomb had dropped.

'They go,' said Burke with a grin. 'Two dozen like that and then we can call it finished.'

Red flame was spurting out now, very vivid against the snow. Smoke was like a cloud over the earth. Here and there a square mile of land seemed to burst, first in smoke, then in flame.

'So,' said Burke, 'they had some powder down there, and one or two live shells. Pity, isn't it? It's taken Krotz years to get all that stuff ready, and now it's going to vanish in a few short hours.'

'Sure,' said Bob Carruthers, 'it's a shame. How many more?'

'Three,' said Burke.

It looked so simple from the plane. The last bomb fell on a tank of nitro-glycerine, although they didn't know it, and set the seal on that ten minutes of destruction.

Below, fire was raging, tons of high explosives were going up every second, underground stores were caving in, petrol was exploding. Twenty miles of Lathia was nothing but fire and smoke and living death.

Burke said:

'Better get across to Sweden now. They're the most neutral people I know, and we'll be able to get a message to London. Craigie might be able to do something even now.'

Carruthers nodded.

The machine turned towards the West, and the pall of smoke passed beneath them. They were flying high, and Rikka was only just visible, a little white mound on a flat white earth.

22

A VOICE ACROSS THE WORLD

The offices of the Enterprise Assurance Company were taken over by the police, and each member of the staff questioned and cross-examined. Very little resulted. The company was a small one, but it had been established for over fifty years, and the two directors emphatically denied any knowledge of the activities of their Personal Policy Manager. But they did admit that they had been in financial difficulties, and that only heavy backing from the firm of Smethwick and Karen had saved them. Yes, the man Sutton—as they knew him—had not been with the company many months, and he had come with a strong recommendation from Nathaniel Smethwick. He had, moreover, replaced a younger manager named Bray, who had also been introduced by Smethwick. Bray, it was understood, had taken a staff position in the London office of Smethwick and Karen.

So much, then, was understood.

Craigie learned more as the examination of the papers and documents in the Personal Policy office proceeded. A surprising number of policies covered gentlemen from the

East, and gradually the thing took shape. The policies were guarantees from Krotz to the Eastern Powers. Under the guise of private insurance the messages had gone from West to East. The system of communication had been infallible. Craigie admitted it.

Rumours of the conflagration in Europe were spreading, and the English Cabinet was in permanent session. Emergency military measures were started. Craigie was called to No. 10. What did he advise? He had his finger on the pulse of things.

Craigie said:

'Go to the League.'

'But the League can't help,' they told him.

'Nothing else can,' said Craigie. 'The European fire must be put out, gentlemen, or before we know where we are we'll have the Eastern invasion cutting across the Continent. *Go to the League!* Let the East know we are prepared, and are expecting them. Tell them the West is united, not divided. That might frighten them; nothing else will. And it won't help, coming from Great Britain, it must come from the League.'

Few of the men present had the same trust in the League that Craigie had, but they agreed. A certain Prelate, President of the League Council, talked with Craigie. Messages flashed anew, from East to West and back again, but the East's replies were uncompromising. The invasion had started. A mutiny in the Greek Navy, fomented by Eastern agitators, left a dozen cruisers in the hands of the holiday-makers in the Mediterranean, and Greece became the starting point of the assault on Europe. The East believed that the nations of the West were fighting amongst themselves, and that the invasion would succeed because of that.

Apart from the Greek mutiny, there had been no real disclosure of Western activities, and Craigie saw a slight chance of evading catastrophe, but none of avoiding war. The only chance was to unite Europe—a Europe that was inflamed with internal passion, whose nations were marching against each other.

The stupendous cleverness of it sickened Craigie.

It sickened the League, but no one stopped working. Berlin was temporarily pacified, after the attack on the Leader. Paris, despite the destruction of a frontier town by what seemed to be German planes, agreed to delay action. Neither Power would have stopped but for the urgent warning of the threat from the East. But if the big Powers were resting on their arms, the smaller countries were itching to get at each other. Even Lathia, the good boy of Europe, had gone mad, and the Balkan explosion had come again.

And then Craigie had the message from Burke, who talked from Sweden over the long-distance line. He said:

'Krotz is dead, and the arms factory is up in smoke. The invaders will get no help from Lathia. If you can convince them, it might make the East call a halt.'

'I'll try,' said Craigie. 'Good man, Burke. Get back as soon as you can.'

He turned from the telephone and set the machine of international communication going. The East refused, at first, to believe it. Then their own spies sent urgent messages, mostly now from the West to the East.

The voice of the League went across the world. The East acknowledged it at last, knowing that it was complete withdrawal or complete annihilation, for without the arms from Lathia the invading forces were helpless!

The Government forces in Greece took control again. European cruisers surrounded certain pleasure liners in Western seas, for there was time now; and the liners steamed towards the East. The trans-Russian railway, which had carried an army to within three hundred miles of Lathia, was taken over by the Soviet, and the army went back to Manchuria, Mongolia and Sinkiang.

There was a flare-up in Europe, but only rumours of the invasion from the East; and of course, those rumours were scoffed at by the clever.

Burke and Carruthers reached London on the following day and were interviewed by Men Who Mattered until they were sick of it. Burke finally told them he was too tired to say more and went to see Craigie at the Department Z office. Carruthers, with a touch of fever, was taken to hospital.

Craigie was looking greyer than usual, but he was still smoking his pipe.

'Dane and Curtis?' he asked.

Burke drummed on the arms of his chair.

'Gone,' he said. 'No chance at all.' There was silence for a minute, before he went on: 'What happened over here?'

Craigie told him of the Enterprise Company, and its records.

'It wasn't safe for Krotz to be in communication with the East,' he said. 'We'd have learned of it. But he was in touch here and the Enterprise Company made contact for him.'

Burke nodded.

'We saved Cassey,' said Craigie. 'The man Lister, who followed you some time back, tried to get him. But Miller had warned the Scottish police, and they caught him. He's the only one alive, I think. A young man—Bray—probably the man who killed Karen.'

Burke nodded.

'He came to the Enterprise office,' said Craigie, 'and shot

himself when he saw what had happened. Lister's willing to talk—by the way, Rogers died from his injuries—but he doesn't know much. Only that Bray and Smethwick organised the Cannon Street raid, and the poor devil Sutton—the real Sutton was an accountant in the Newcastle works of Smethwick and Karen—was killed as Smethwick. Bilton, Cassey, and everyone who knew Smethwick were to go too.'

'To keep Smethwick safe,' muttered Burke. 'When did he start in it? Do you know?'

'Right from the beginning, according to Lister. He shipped a lot of steel across to Lathia. The Newcastle firm owed its success to that and, of course, Smethwick had to see it through, or take a chance of disclosure.'

Burke nodded.

'I've heard from the woman Day,' said Gordon Craigie, with a ghost of a smile. 'She told me she'd sent you to Wembley, and why. She knew you weren't in the regular police—and she and her husband . . .'

'Husband?'

'Yes,' said Craigie. 'Their real name is Rannigan, but we may as well use the name we know. The genuine Hemming is somewhere in Europe, for his health. Anyhow, she thought it safer to talk to you than to the police, and she guessed, after the murder at Hampstead, that Miss Carris was in danger. So she sent you there.'

'Bless her,' murmured Burke.

Craigie nodded and smiled.

'The real Smethwick murdered Sutton,' went on Craigie. 'And that's pretty well all of it, Burke. Hemming, alias Rannigan, is getting a free passage back to America, with his wife. The only crimes they committed, if they were crimes, was getting Miss Carris down from Scotland, and then holding out on what they knew. You can't blame them, for they didn't have much chance of getting out of the murder charge, as things were.'

'They didn't,' admitted Burke, thinking of the suave, grey-haired man who had entered the hall at Hampstead. Hemming had been drawn into the affair without realising its seriousness. A polished confidence trickster with a pretty wife, to whom Patricia Carris owed her life. For if Smethwick had reached the Wembley house before Burke had done, Patricia would have had little chance. Krotz hadn't doubted Burke's loyalty. If he had, if Burke had died, Europe would have been Europe in name only. Or if Carris hadn't taken the chance of telling Burke the truth, the invasion must have come about.

Craigie tapped his pipe.

'I've heard from the Arrans,' he said. 'Toby is on the mend, Tim's still in a bad way, but he'll pull through. There was a raid on the *Vissen*. The papers were taken. So if it hadn't been for the discovery of the Enterprise Company, Krotz would have waited for a little longer and preparations would have been even more complete. You pulled it off, Burke.'

Jim Burke stretched his big frame and grinned.

'Why not?' he asked. 'It's what I'm for.'

'And now,' said Craigie, with a ghost of a smile, 'I suppose you're going to have a nice long holiday.'

Burke stopped smiling.

'Gordon,' he said, 'there's a hell of a lot to do before I take a holiday. You're thinking of Pat and me, of course. Well—one day, I hope. But not yet. You can use me, can't you?'

Craigie thought of the madness in Europe and other places, and he said, very quietly:

'You will be invaluable, Jim.'

The two men shook hands.

'But you'll lay off for a few weeks,' said the Chief of

Department Z. 'The only man who can do much, at the moment, is the Prelate.'

'The League,' murmured Burke. 'Do you think it will gain control now?'

'I just hope,' said Craigie. 'I just hope.'

His hopes were justified. Slowly the fire in Europe died down. There were flare-ups in small countries, and there was bitter feeling between Powers, but they had had time to see the madness of war, just then. So there was no war.

A very big man, with dark crisp hair, and a smaller man, with fair hair and a perpetual smile, landed at Southampton six months after they had dropped bombs on the arms factory in Lathia. They had been busy, and they knew a great many more things about the situation in Europe than they had done a year before. In due course they made their reports to Gordon Craigie. And then they walked towards Piccadilly, from Whitehall.

Craigie had told them a lot of things, and Burke was still thinking of them. He learned, for instance, that the driver of the lorry that had killed one man and wounded Wally Davidson had been found and had confessed. He had been one of Karen's gang, but had worked under orders from Number 3 when committing the outrage.

He had worked with Gustav Hermann and the gunmen at Wembley. All of them had other crimes to answer for, besides their share in the Karen murders.

From Hermann, Craigie had learned that Karen handled the business between Smethwick and Karen and their imaginary Lathian factory and that the gang had been organised to cover emergencies. All the time Karen and Smethwick had risked discovery, and in the gunmen they had a quick answer to any attempts to stop them. It was Hermann who told them, too, that Sutton, the accountant from Newcastle, had discovered that Smethwick was using his name, and had threatened trouble. Smethwick had lured him to the Hampstead house and murdered him.

And that, thought Burke grimly, was the end of it. Then he smiled. There was one thing Craigie had told him that had reminded him very vividly of those two small but pugnacious men, the Arrans. Timothy and Tobias had stolen papers from the Villa Krotz that recorded the instructions sent from Krotz to the Personal Policy Manager of the Enterprise Company. But for the collision at sea, the Arrans might have played a bigger part in the final round up.

Carruthers grinned suddenly, and knocked Burke's arm.

They were approaching the doors of the Carilon Club, and they saw two small, well-dressed men come out of it, one with the face of an angel and the other with the ugliest features in London. The two men stopped and beamed as Burke and Carruthers reached them.

'Ho, Burke!'

Jim Burke smiled delightedly.

'If it isn't Tim and Toby,' he said, as they shook hands. 'Do they still sell beer in this place?'

'Come and see,' said Timothy Arran.

'Me, too?' asked Carruthers modestly.

'Bring the whole world,' said Timothy generously. 'We want to tell you a little bit about a hot-spot called the Dalinka.'

Just an hour afterwards Jim Burke reached his furnished flat in Brook Street. He was alone, for the fair-headed Carruthers was telling the Arrans what fine lads they were, and the Arrans were agreeing with enthusiasm. The door of the flat opened before Burke reached it, and a sturdy man dressed in navy blue greeted him with unashamed delight.

'Ain't I glad to see you, Mr. Burke!'

Burke shook hands with a certain Mr. Peter Carter.

'Hallo, Sam!' he said, grinning. 'Reformed, Sam, or hankering after the good old days?'

'Bless yer, Mr. Burke, I ain't been so 'appy in all me natteral. Say, listen, yer'll 'ave to 'urry. Miss Patricia reckons she'll be round in 'alf an hour.'

Burke bathed and changed into clothes neatly laid out by Carter, who confessed that he had been taking lessons, and who led his employer to a table set for two.

'All me own work,' he said proudly.

'Splendid,' enthused Burke. 'Ah . . .'

There was a knock at the door.

Patricia came, looking cool and beautiful, and without the shadows in her eyes. They hugged and kissed and then they talked of the day they hoped would come. If she had not been the sister of Nick Carris, she might not have understood why that day was still far distant. But she did understand.

There was work for Burke to do.

ABOUT THE AUTHOR

John Creasey, born in 1908, was a paramount English crime and science fiction writer who used myriad pseudonyms for more than six hundred novels. He founded the UK Crime Writers' Association in 1953. In 1962, his book *Gideon's Fire* received the Edgar Award for Best Novel from the Mystery Writers of America. Many of the characters featured in Creasey's titles became popular, including George Gideon of Scotland Yard, who was the basis for a subsequent television series and film. Creasey died in Salisbury, UK, in 1973.

DEPARTMENT Z

FROM OPEN ROAD MEDIA

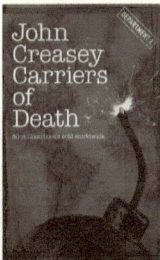